Deep in the Night

An Alexander Ranch Matter # 3

By Marla Josephs

Cover photo by Beverly Fields and Amado Temporal

© Tempfield Press and Beverly Fields 2014

To my husband, my partner in all things. Thanks for everything. You are the best. And to my children, you are my inspiration.

Prologue

"Come here, doggy."

The dog came warily closer to the hand holding out a piece of bread.

"That's it. Come on," the soothing voice crooned.

Finally deciding that everything was safe, the dog gave into his desire for the bread and gradually took it from the outstretched hand. After gulping that piece down in one bite, the dog was handed another and another. When all the bread was gone, the dog lay down and allowed the stranger to pet his head. He soon grew sleepy and fell into a deep, soothing sleep. The next morning when the dog's owner called to him, he did not respond.

"Bear! Bear!" the boy called out over and over again. But, Bear did not come. When the boy finally walked around to the side of the house where the dog run was, he saw the dog lying on the ground sleeping. That was odd, thought the boy. Bear wasn't usually asleep at this time. And, even if he was, he would have awakened at hearing his name. The boy sank down next to the dog and pet him gently along his back. Then he stiffened. Something was very wrong. Bear's body felt deathly still.

"Bear?" the boy said placing his hand on the animal's side and then quickly drawing it away. He stood up so abruptly he stumbled backward.

"Mom! M-o-o-o-m! Something's wrong with Bear!" he yelled as he ran towards the house. Bear lay still, never to move again.

Chapter 1

Why is it that the first days back from a vacation are always the busiest? Yet, they are probably the days you are least mentally prepared for work? I was now sitting in my office after a long day reminiscing about the relaxing vacation I'd just had. Prior to said vacation, I'd had a long, back and forth debate with myself about where to go on vacation. In the end, my brother Blake and I had agreed to an all-inclusive, eight day vacation in Puerta Vallarta, Mexico. Blake had originally left the decision to me. However, he'd had to step in when I couldn't seem to make up my mind. We ended up agreeing that we wanted something like a staycation…just not at home.

Though Puerta Vallarta had a lot to do, we'd been there several times before. Hanging out at the pool, relaxing, eating, and snoozing in the Mexican shade sounded just fine for now. If we had gone somewhere else, we wouldn't have been able to force ourselves to relax. Blake, however, was tired of travelling and didn't want to spend his vacation going on excursion after excursion each day. He travelled constantly for work, and I simply worked all the time. We needed a restful vacation.

So, we had a nice, relaxing vacation with only a few excursions. Blake parasailed one afternoon from the beach in front of our resort while I videotaped. Our busiest day was the second day we were there. We decided to do two excursions on the same day. We swam with the dolphins by day and enjoyed a rousing pirate dinner cruise on the Marigalante by night. Swimming with the dolphins was always so much fun. It just wouldn't have been complete without that and the Marigalante.

The Marigalante is an exact replica of Columbus' Santa Maria. Besides the beautiful views of Puerto Vallarta and Banderas Bay from the ship, the crew put on a heck of a pirate show. The entertainment included one of the performers diving off the ship into the water in the dark of night and a fireworks show. The food wasn't too shabby either. Actually, it was downright delicious. No matter how many times we visited Puerta Vallarta, we never missed these two excursions. They were a must do.

The only other excursion we had was a trip to do some shopping. For Blake and I, that was probably the most subdued vacation we'd ever been on. And now, I was back at work wishing that I'd booked it for a little longer and taken just a few more days off. Perhaps I was becoming less of a workaholic.

Being on vacation had been a heck of a lot better than trying to figure out what was going on with our client's animals. Several of our clients had brought their dogs to us close to death, or dead, with no obvious cause of death. None of them had survived. We probably wouldn't have thought much of it if only one or two clients had come in. But, apparently these mysterious deaths had started while I was on vacation. In the last nine days, five cases had found their way to our veterinary clinic.

After being investigated by our vet staff, poisoning was ruled out via blood tests. Each owner had been question regarding the food they fed their pets. Each dog was fed a different brand of food according to the owners, which ruled out a food born outbreak from a specific manufacturer. Currently we were stumped. Now, we were contemplating having the bodies sent out for necropsy or sending out tissue samples to determine some other toxicological reason. For now, we were advising our pet owners to keep a close eye on their pets and keep their animals with them at all times. Realizing I was now frowning at my latest thoughts about our suspicious pet deaths, I moved to shut my computer down just as my phone rang. It was Jordan.

Jordan was my…boyfriend? We hadn't exactly defined our relationship. After a rocky beginning that included me getting shot, him saving me, some hot steamy kisses mixed with a lot of reluctance on my part, we finally settled on dating.

"Hey," I said smiling in anticipation of his voice. I hadn't heard that voice in almost two weeks while I was on vacation. I'd missed it.

"I missed you," he said in his low, rich tone. That tone that never failed to cause the flutters in my stomach.

"I missed you too," I said impishly. I knew what was coming next, and I was trying to hide my laughter in anticipation.

"Are you sure, Lela?" he asked, his voice taking on a tone that was a cross between disgruntled and sarcastic. "You didn't call me when you got in last night like I asked you to."

"It was late, Jordan," I said trying to reason with him. I really had missed Jordan. But, I'd been exhausted when Blake and I had returned late. And, if I had called Jordan to let him know I was home, he'd have shown up on my doorstep, or more accurately, in my bed. I was half surprised I hadn't found him there this morning.

"I told you I didn't care what time you got in. I would have still come over," he explained earnestly.

"I know, Jordan," I groaned. "That's what I was afraid of."

"See, I knew you didn't miss me," he feigned a pout.

"I did. I told you so this morning when I texted you that I was on my way to work," I chided. "I was really tired. We got in really late. If you had come over, I wouldn't have gotten enough sleep to get to work this morning."

"You're always tired," he commented grumpily. "You need some Geritol or something."

"Oh…, wow. Thanks!" I shot back sardonically. "I'm so sorry I don't have super human energy and strength like you. How dare I need eight hours of sleep regularly."

"Seriously, Lela. You sleep more than the average person," he went on, warming to his topic.

"Uh, Jordan?"

"Hm?" came his smug voice.

"I'm thinking maybe you don't get to come over tonight either," I said sweetly.

"Ok, ok. I'm just messing with you," he said easily. "Are you headed home now?"

"I just shut my computer down."

"I'll meet you there."

Blake wasn't home when I arrived, but Jordan was sitting in the driveway in his Aston Martin when I pulled in. I'd barely turned the engine off before he was there opening my door with a big grin on his face. The moment I was out of the car he pulled me into his arms for an urgent kiss. As usual, that was all it took for me to melt into him.

"We are going to dinner," he announced in a voice that brooked no argument when he finally released my mouth. "Do you need to change clothes or anything?"

I didn't. I was the Facilities Director for Hanley's Pet Care Services. Although I was a registered vet tech, I almost never worked in that capacity. My job was to make all of the various departments run smoothly at our facilities. We had pet grooming, training, boarding and veterinary care services. I made it all work seamlessly for the needs of our clients. Since I'd been buried by all of the paperwork that went along with my job today, I hadn't had a moment to even visit the actual facilities where animal interaction took place. Being animal hair and germ free, there was no need for me to change.

"Actually, I'm starving. And, no. I don't need to change clothes. I'll just text Blake on the way and let him know I've gone out to dinner with you."

I hit the button on the key fob to lock my car and climbed into the passenger side of his car where Jordan was holding the door for me.

"The Aston Martin tonight?" I asked with a raised brow when he climbed in beside me on the driver's side.

"You are mine tonight," he stated and then frowned. "Well, at least you are for a little while. I know you won't come back to the ranch with me, and I know you won't be totally mine tonight at your house with Blake there. So, I figured, I'd take you to dinner to get you to myself for a few hours."

"Sounds good," I laughed. "Just remember it's a work night."

"Don't worry. I'll have you home in time to get your beauty rest," he teased.

Jordan pulled up in front of our favorite Italian restaurant right on the water. My stomach grumbled loudly and my mouth began to water.

"Il Pescatore?" I asked excitedly.

"I knew you'd like this," Jordan said smugly.

"Heck yea!" I exclaimed enthusiastically. "You have to make sure I save room for the tiramisu."

"If you don't, we can always take it to go," he shrugged with a knowing grin.

My hunger pangs became more insistent once we entered the restaurant and all of the wonderful smells teased my nose.

"So, how was your first day back?" Jordan asked once we were seated.

"Busy!" I declared. "And, I was *so* not into it today. Though, I had no choice but to make myself dive in head first. There's so much to do. And, we've got a problem that we can't seem to figure out."

"What kind of problem?" Jordan murmured looking over the menu.

"Apparently, while I was gone, several clients brought their dogs in wondering why their previously healthy dogs seemed to just drop dead. Looking over their records, all of them came in for their regular checkups and were in great shape. None of the prior exams indicated these dogs were anything but healthy."

"What do you mean, just dropped dead?" Jordan asked looking up from his menu.

"I mean, they just dropped dead," I exclaimed definitively. "Each of the owners just found their dog dead, or close to it, in the morning. No wounds, evidence of a fight, or injury. If it had been one or two then we'd have assumed it was a coincidence."

"How many have there been?" Jordan was now looking very interested.

"Apparently, there have been five in the last nine days. And, one more came in today. It's crazy. We were starting to suspect that someone might be poisoning them. John approved the vets doing blood work to test for poison while I was gone. The results came back today and there is no sign of poisoning. We just can't figure it out. We are thinking of sending them out for some necropsies, or at least checking the tissues for other toxicology or organ failure."

Jordan was looking thoughtful. Before I could question him, however, our waitress came to take our orders. I ordered a much needed glass of wine along with a seafood ravioli entre. Jordan ordered a combination platter that he would undoubtedly eat every bite of and still have room for dessert.

"So, there haven't been any clear signs of cause of death? No evidence of any type of fight or struggle?" Jordan asked, repeating my words once the waitress walked away to put our orders in.

"No. Nothing. According to each of the owners, the dogs seemed to just be sleeping peacefully."

"Do you think Grace could take a look at the corpses?" Jordan was frowning now. His question had me almost choking on my water. "Grace? Why?"

"I don't know," he said pensively. "We've caught a case that we are finding rather strange as well. They don't seem to be related, yet I feel like we should check it out."

"What kind of case?"

"We've had two men drained very violently in the last week and a half. And, while this isn't necessarily an unusual occurrence, they were both found dead in their cars not very far away from each other. We don't know where they were drained, but they don't have anything in common. And, they didn't live anywhere near each other, or where they were dumped. Normally a drainer would not bother to drive their victims anywhere after killing them. At most, they would make only minimal effort to hide the body."

"So, you think my dead dogs might have something to do with your dead men?" I asked skeptically.

"No, not necessarily. However, it sounds like your dogs may have been drained. So, we should probably not overlook these strange deaths. It's still an unusual death for a drained dog. Most drainers who kill animals don't care if they brutally drain them. They usually wouldn't do it close enough to their homes to leave the bodies where the owners could find them. Like you said, maybe if it were one here and there it wouldn't be cause for suspicion. But, five dogs killed the same way in a matter of days is a pattern."

Our waitress brought our food then, cutting off our conversation.

"Enough shop talk," Jordan said once our waitress walked away. "Tell me all about Mexico and how you were too busy to even miss me."

"I wasn't too busy to miss you," I laughed. "Actually, I missed you very much."

"Sure," Jordan grumbled pretending disbelief. "Just tell me about all the fun you had."

Throughout the rest of dinner I told Jordan about the relaxing time I had in Mexico. He seemed genuinely interested.

Did I mention that Jordan was part of, what I called, a super human group called drainers? Drainers survived by draining the very life force of living things. Jordan's brother, Logan, was married to another such super human named Grace. Only, Grace was a healer and a medically certified physician. She could literally touch a person and heal them.

According to the Alexander clan, drainers and healers living together was unusual. They weren't usually two groups that spent a lot of time with each other. Jordan and his brother, and a few other drainers that worked with the Alexanders, did not sustain themselves by killing people or animals for their life force. Instead they had a whole ranch of animals that they randomly pulled small quantities of life force from when necessary. And, they absolutely never touched the life force of other humans. According to Jordan, the life force of a human was known to become addicting to their kind if touched.

What I discovered on my first encounter with the animals of Alexander Ranch was that their animals where somehow healthier and more robust than normal. It was almost as if having their life forces touched regularly, but to no major degree, caused them to become stronger. I thought of it like a muscle. When lifting weights there are tiny injuries that happen to the muscle. However, after the muscle works to repair itself, the end result is stronger muscles. This is how the animals of Alexander Ranch were. The animals tended to live longer and remain healthy and fit throughout their lives.

Jordan, Logan, and the few other drainers that worked for Alexander Ranch were unfortunately the exception when it came to drainers being good guys. They made quite a nice living bringing other drainers to justice for the crimes of murder, theft, and whatever else their kind did. In possession of super human strength, no other law enforcement agency or group could possible contain them, nor did they know of the existence of the particular breed of human the Alexanders were members of. I was one of the few, thanks to my almost being killed by walking into a drainer crime in the making, to know of the existence of these people.

Jordan insisted that they were still people, just people with a few extra abilities. I couldn't argue the point, because he likened it to my own ability. I was definitely nothing more than a regular old human. A normal, as the Alexanders called everyone who wasn't a drainer or a healer. My only extra ability was telepathy. I was only just starting to explore this ability due to the Alexanders. Upon discovering my ability, they asked for my help in solving a case. And, I finally found value in my gift when it helped a great deal in bringing a kidnapped victim home to his family. My gift was still a heavily guarded secret. I just didn't try to hide it from myself anymore.

After our dinner Jordan drove me home and groaned as he pulled to the curb in front of my house.

"What?" I asked trying to understand why his jovial demeanor was taking on a sour look.

"Daisy and Ethan are here," he practically grumbled. I smiled. Daisy was Jordan's sister in law. Her sister, Grace, was married to Jordan's brother, Logan. Ethan was the cousin of Daisy and Grace.

"Blake is here too," I pointed out, gesturing to my brother's car in the driveway next to mine. "It's not like we would have been alone."

"Yes, but, if Blake were home alone he might have been in his room. Then I could sneak in your room undetected."

"Come on," I said shaking my head as I climbed out of the car. Jordan snuck in my room undetected all of the time. That was another trait he had. He could get in and out of places as quiet as a cat burglar. Locks were not a deterrent, nor were security systems. With his exceptional vision and hearing he was never caught. Luckily he was one of the good guys.

We entered the house to see Ethan, Blake and Daisy all watching a baseball game. There were pizza boxes and beer bottles on the family room coffee table.

"Hey, Lela! How was your trip?" Daisy asked jumping up to give me a big hug. She continued speaking before I could answer her. "I'm so glad to have you back. I didn't have anyone but the guys to hang out with. As you see, they have me drinking beer and watching sports."

"Hi, Daisy," I chuckled.

"Seriously. I missed you."

"I missed you too," I said still grinning at her. "But, I was relaxing and enjoying myself in Mexico."

"Next time, I'm going with you," she stated.

"Actually that would be fun," I nodded.

"Hey, sexy woman," Ethan said, edging Daisy aside so that he could pick me up, swing me around in a hug, and then give me a big, smacking kiss on the lips. Ethan lived and worked with the Alexander's at the ranch. He also loved to try and get under Jordan's skin by flirting outrageously with me. He put me down and shot a mischievous grin at Jordan.

"Babe, you don't know where his lips have been. Don't let him do that," Jordan said frowning at me as he flipped Ethan off. "Since Ethan can't seem to find his own woman, and he can't have you, who knows what he's using as a substitute for love and affection."

"Ok! That's enough strange maleness," Daisy said holding up a hand to each of them before turning to me. "See what I mean? I'm surrounded by testosterone."

"I know you guys just ate, but there's plenty of pizza," Blake offered as he tried to smother a laugh. He really enjoyed the Alexanders and their antics. Ethan, Jordan, Daisy and I spent a lot of time together. And though Blake travelled a lot for work, whenever he was home the Alexander clan was there. So, they'd become just as much his friends as mine. I was stuffed, but I wasn't at all surprised that Jordan seemed to have room for pizza and beer. The Alexanders could pack it in.

After the game, Jordan left with Daisy and Ethan. I knew he'd be back though. Part of the reason for his departure was for Blake's sake. He didn't want Blake to know he'd be spending the night in my room. The other reason, I suspected, was because he needed to inform Logan, Grace and the others about the dead dogs. I verified my suspicions when Jordan entered my room from the darkened hallway. He'd sent me a text advising me that he was coming so he wouldn't scare the bejeezers out of me.

"So, did you inform everyone about the dogs?" I asked as he climbed into the bed next to me.

"I did," he said pulling the covers over us and wrapping his arms around my waist. He propped himself up on his elbow and looked down at me. "Logan was very interested, as was everyone else. I still can't see how it could be connected. They can't either. Yet, we were all still compelled to check it out."

"Yea, it doesn't make sense that a drainer would brutally drain two men, yet gently drain five dogs," I frowned up at him puzzled. I was lying on my back and trying not to be effected by the slow circles his thumb was making on my hip.

"Well, we know it was the same drainer who killed both of the men," Jordan said. "We'll know soon enough if it was the same one who drained the dogs."

"How will you know that?"

"The smell," Jordan said tapping the side of his nose cheekily. Of course. Why hadn't I thought of that? "The scent of the drainer was easily detected on our two victims. From the scent on the dogs, we'll know it either is or isn't the same person."

"Who detected the smell?" I shuddered at the idea of having to identify someone by sniffing a dead body. The very idea of having to deal with the dead body of a murder victim was enough to make me squeamish.

16

"Grace, of course," Jordan smirked, clearly reading my thoughts in my face. "She's the doctor, though, any of us could have done it."

Jordan bent down and brushed a brief kiss along my lips. After lingering for a few moments he raised his head and spoke again.

"Speaking of dead bodies, Logan would like you to help us out with some interviews. Do you think you can make the time?"

"I should be able to as long as we schedule them. How many do you need?" I asked. I had a feeling this would come up again sooner or later. In their previous investigation, the Alexanders had me sit in on interviews and interrogations so that I could read the thoughts of the suspects or other persons of interest. My job was to report the reactions and responses that the person being interviewed did not say or show.

"I'm not really sure," he said and stopped for a moment to nip my bottom lip. "And, how soon do you think Grace can take a look at your dogs?"

"I can get her in tomorrow, or anytime," I said, my voice sounding raspy now with desire.

"I'll let her know. I'll also let Logan know you are on board for the interviews," he said and then gently rolled over on top of me, pinning me to the bed.

"Jordan," I hissed in warning. Jordan had made a habit of climbing into my bed with me at night for the last two weeks

17

before my vacation. I'd warned him not to make a habit of this, but he seemed inclined to ignore my warning.

"Yes, Lela?" he asked in his husky voice before capturing my lips with his. As usual, I melted before my brain had a chance to catch up with my body. After a long moment, I turned my head breaking the kiss. That was when he began nibbling on my neck in the spot he knew drove me crazy while his hand slipped under my tank top and caressed my breast. I sighed. I loved the feel of Jordan's weight on me, his hands on me, and that very naughty mouth on me. It wasn't until his free hand began making its way south and under the elastic of my shorts I wore to sleep, that I finally heeded the alarm bells going off in my head.

"Jordan!" My voice came out in a breathy whisper as I grabbed his hand.

"Ah, come on, Lela," he crooned against my neck kissing and then nipping.

"Blake is home," I said in a strained whisper. I feebly and ineffectively pushed against his shoulders. "No."

Technically, I lived with my brother, Blake. After college, I'd moved in with him to be his roommate. Only, he travelled a lot for work, so he was gone more than he was home. He wouldn't let me pay for anything besides my personal bills because, he claimed he should be paying me for house sitting. Otherwise his house would sit vacant most of the time. So, I basically lived alone in my brother's house except for on the few occasions, maybe once or twice a month for a weekend, that my brother visited his home.

I'd already gotten lost in the bliss of what Jordan was doing to me until his words reminded me that I was supposed to be keeping things from going too far tonight.

"Blake won't know," he said finally, thankfully lifting his head from my neck to frown down at me. "Well, if you just be quiet he won't know anything."

"Jordan Alexander, If you don't behave I am kicking you out!" I said in my sternest stage whisper under the circumstances. He frowned down at me and I frowned back. At least I tried to frown back. After a brief stare down he rolled off of me and on to his side with a frustrated sigh.

"You're killing me," he groaned.

"Hey, you can always go home," I said and smacked him on the arm. "I'm not forcing you to stay here. As a matter of fact, I seem to remember telling you not to make a habit of crawling into my bed at night. You have a perfectly good one at the ranch."

"Yes, but you aren't in it," he said in a tone that sounded like a borderline whine.

"And, I'm not going to be," I insisted with a little more conviction. "That would be worse than here with your supersonic hearing family."

"This is worse than when we first met," he complained.

"What are you talking about?" I snorted. "You barely spoke to me from a distance, let alone got close enough to touch me."

"No. When we first met, if you want to call it that, you were unconscious and I was holding you in my arms," he grinned and rolled over settling his weight on me again. "I'd been terrified of hurting you, but it hadn't stopped me from wanting you. I'd had to strip you naked practically and sit in that warm tub of water with you."

"Ok. Let's not have a flashback," I said feeling embarrassed. I'd forgotten about that. Or rather, I hadn't thought much of it. Considering I had been unconscious most of that time, there wasn't as much for me to remember. "I remembered being attracted to you too. But, then you turned into a horse's ass once we were away from there."

I'd basically washed up on the beach, where Jordan had been sitting alone, after I'd jumped into the river to get away from some men who I'd just witnessed shooting Ethan. Because they saw me and knew I'd seen what they'd done, they wanted to kill me too. It was a traumatic day.

"You were attracted to me then, huh?" he asked looking pleased and naughty as he moved against me shooting heat straight to my loins.

"Once I realized you weren't going to kill me, hadn't molested me, at least I didn't think you had, and got over being embarrassed at finding myself redressed and sleeping next to a strange man? Yea, it dawned on me that you were sort of attractive," I teased.

"I didn't molest you in any way, though I wanted to. I just wanted to touch you," he said sliding a hand down my left thigh and then lifting it to pull my leg around him. "But, besides the fact that you were hurt and I was terrified you might die on me, I wasn't sure that I could touch you without hurting you. I wasn't sure if my attraction to you was based on your sheer hotness, or if I was also attracted to your life force. Not ever being attracted to one of you normals before, I just didn't know."

"So, you've never been attracted to one of us normals?" I asked skeptically, trying to ignore the way he was making me go up in flames rocking against me. My breathing was speeding up and my words came out breathy, betraying my lack of calm. "But, I thought we weren't so different than you guys besides the super power stuff."

"Oh, I've seen some very attractive normal women. But, I can't say I was ever attracted to them. Probably because I've never spent any real time around them," he said trying to sound casual. However, the heat in his eyes and the hardness I felt pressing into me through my clothes betrayed him. He was definitely not unaffected. "But, something about you just drew me in."

"Don't think I don't know what you are doing." I narrowed my eyes at him.

"What?" he asked trying to play innocent. I pushed at him and he rolled over.

"That's better," I giggled.

"You know," Jordan said thoughtfully as he propped himself on his elbow to look down at me. "Grace and Logan had their bedroom walls sound proofed so that even we can't hear what they do in there. So did my parents, thank heaven. I could always-"

"No! I am not going to your house and sleeping with you in your bed. You have two choices," I said and ticked them off. "You can take your horny self-home and sleep in your own bed-"

"That's not going to happen," he murmured against my mouth. I ignored him.

"Or, you can go to sleep."

"You are no fun," he said wrinkling his nose at me. "You know I could convince you if I wanted to."

I did know that all too well. I was just hoping he didn't know just how easily he could have me throwing caution to the wind and giving in to this uncontrollable desire that seemed to be between us.

"But, you won't," I said firmly and turned my back to him. He threw an arm around me and pulled me in closer. I could feel his erection pressing against me. Thankfully Jordan fell asleep, as men do, very quickly. Somehow I managed to do the same a while later.

Chapter 2

The first thing I did when I arrived in my office the next morning was leave John, the owner and my boss, a message that I would be at the veterinary facility for the morning. I went on to explain that the Alexanders had experienced a similar situation to the one we were with the dead dogs, and Grace wanted to view the bodies we currently had of the deceased dogs. Grace being a medical doctor, I was pretty sure John wouldn't mind. I told him that I would be there to show her the bodies and the records of tests performed on each dog so that I wouldn't have to interrupt the vet staff.

I knew Grace wanted to view the bodies only to determine if they'd been drained, and if the perpetrator was the same as the one who had killed the two men. But, John wouldn't know anything about that.

I had a main office that was strictly mine in the training and boarding facility. However, in each of the other facilities, there was a smaller office that John and I shared. We called these the community offices. We were rarely at the same location at the same time, so this worked out. I was at the veterinary facility today, so I was using the community office.

"Hey Lela," Chris said from the doorway just as I was hanging up the phone. Chris was one of the receptionists at the veterinary facility and always had a bubbly smile. "The Alexanders are here."

"Thanks, Chris," I smiled back at her and stood. "Send them in."

Since Chris had said the Alexanders and not just Grace, I assumed the clan didn't want to be left out of the loop until the meeting that evening. Sure enough, Jordan and Ethan followed Grace into the office.

"I see the guys wouldn't let you come alone," I teased after all of the greetings and hugs were done. Jordan hadn't spoken but came to stand beside me once I was done greeting everyone else. He slid an arm around my waist and gave my temple a quick kiss before releasing me.

"Of course not. We haven't seen you in almost two weeks," Logan smiled. "How was Mexico?"

"Wonderful," I responded wistfully.

"Blake showed us some pictures last night before you and Jordan got in," Ethan informed me. "Looks like you guys had a great time."

"We did," I smiled remembering just how wonderful it had been.

"Well, you'll just have to come over and share the pictures with us," Grace added.

"I've uploaded them online. I'll shoot the album over to you via email," I offered. "We haven't ordered any prints."

"Sounds good," Logan said. "But, you'll still have to come over and tell us about them while we look. How about this evening? We need you to come by to review our case files anyway. We can review the case files, you can stay for dinner, and afterwards, we can check out your vacation."

"I can do that," I agreed. "Speaking of case files. Why don't I show you the dogs first? Then, I'll let you guys have a look at the test results if you want."

"Sounds good," Grace agreed.

I led them down the hall and into the veterinary freezer room where the deceased dogs were located. Several of the dogs had been frozen after tests pending a possible necropsy. The first ones reported, however, had already been picked up for disposal before we realized we were dealing with a possible cause for further investigation. Grace confirmed immediately that the dogs had been drained. And, they all immediately agreed that it was not the same perpetrator who had killed the men. Satisfied that the dogs were not related to their case, Logan suspected that they might have two cases to investigate instead of one.

"Keep me posted, Lela," Logan ordered in his kind way. "Even though this is not the same drainer, we still may have to deal with one who is killing off pets. He might start with dogs and escalate. We still need to keep an eye on this."

"No problem."

"Do you think you can get your morning free tomorrow?" Logan asked. "We could probably be done by around one or one-thirty."

"That shouldn't be a problem. But, why do you need me in the morning?" I asked.

"We need to go interview the co-workers of one of our victims," he explained. We just want you there to make sure we know everything we should. We may have a few more interviews by then too."

"Ok. I'll make myself free for the morning tomorrow," I replied, already planning to bring some work home with me tonight.

"Good. We'll see you this evening then."

I walked them out to Logan's SUV and agreed to come to the ranch directly from work. As Grace, Logan, and Ethan climbed into the car, Jordan pulled me in his arms for a kiss. I put my hands against his chest, intending to limit his public display of affection, but found myself leaning in for his kiss once his lips touched mine.

"She's at work, Jordan," Ethan called out from a backseat window. "Jeeze, show some self-control."

"See you later," Jordan murmured. Then he released me and climbed in the car next to Ethan. From the sound of Grace's stern voice telling them to behave, and Logan's chuckles, I gathered that Ethan was doing his best to needle Jordan. I waved as they drove out of the parking lot and went back inside to finish the rest of my day at work.

Chapter 3

"Maybe we should remove the pictures from the case files," Ethan said dubiously next to me. "She's looking a little green."

I don't know how I looked, but I was certainly feeling a bit queasy. Logan had placed the first case file in front of me and began to go over the case details. However, I hadn't heard a word he'd said. My eyes were glued in horror to the photos before me. The man looked like he'd been beaten to death or something. I couldn't help but wonder if I would have looked like that if the Alexanders hadn't rescued me from a drainer named Kevin.

Kevin had tried to kill me twice. Luckily for me, I had been under the Alexanders' protection at the time. They had rescued me in the nick of time. I still remembered the beating I had taken at his hands as I fought for my life. This victim had obviously not been so lucky.

Suddenly the pictures where snatched from in front of me. I looked up to see Logan placing them face down in front of him and then looking back at me with concern. Ethan wore a similar expression. Everyone else was out on assignment, so Ethan and Logan were filling me in this evening.

"Are you alright?" Logan asked.

"I'm fine," I said feeling a little shaky. "Was he beaten before he was drained?"

"He was definitely in some sort of a fight. He was probably fighting for his life and sustained the injuries you saw,"

Logan explained. "You don't need to see the pictures. We just want you to know the facts surrounding each victim. That way, when we go to interview the families and co-workers, you will know everything we do. And, you'll be able to tell us if something isn't quite right. Maybe there's a connection to the two victims we just haven't uncovered yet, or maybe this guy is a hired killer. We just don't know. So the more you know, the more you will be able to tell us if we stumble across someone who isn't telling us all that they know."

"I'm sorry," I grimaced, feeling a little chagrined. "I was just shocked at seeing the photos. I wasn't expecting that."

"Don't apologize," Logan chided. "We should have thought of that. We are so used to seeing things like this in case files and in person. We should have removed them before."

"Go on. I'm ready," I said with a solemn nod trying frantically to put the ghastly images out of my mind.

"Ok. Victim number one is Elliot Falco. He's a commodities trader. He lives in the gated community here." Logan pointed to a spot on a map posted on the wall. Then he pointed to another location on the map as he spoke his next words. "He works in the city here. He's twenty-six years old, lives alone, and was reported missing after he didn't show up for work the next day, which was eleven days ago."

Logan cocked his head to the side as if puzzled before continuing. Then he pointed to another spot on the map.

"According to the reports," Logan went on, "he was found in his car here. However, from what we can tell, there was no reason for him to be here. It's not near his work or home. From the statement reports that we received from the police, he didn't know anyone in this area, nor did he have any business dealings there. Frankly, it's not far from a pretty bad area. However, everyone the police spoke to said he wasn't into drugs or anything like that. The toxicology report supports that. No one can seem to tell us why he might have been there. But, if he wasn't down there scoring drugs, and didn't know anyone that lived nearby, then we have no idea why he was there."

"We aren't sure where he was actually killed, though," Ethan added. "He wasn't killed in his car. And, so far, no one has found the original crime scene. So, we are thinking he was abducted for some reason other than robbery. His wallet was intact. Unless he had some cash that was stolen, which we wouldn't know about, everything was still there. All of his credit cards and ID were still in his wallet. According to reports, none of his credit card accounts or debit cards showed any activity after the day he went missing."

"The only thing we do know is that our two victims were killed by the same drainer. The smell test confirmed that," Logan said picking up the story. I mused for a moment over how easily they went back and forth with interrogations and such without seeming to notice. "We think that the dump site, so to speak, has more to do with the perpetrator than the victims. The second victim was found not that far away from the first."

Ethan picked up another file, hastily removed the photos, and turned them face down on the table before placing it in front of me. Then he went to stand at the map as he began to speak.

"Victim number two is Peter Dukes. He was forty-five years old, has a wife and two kids, and was a security specialist." Ethan pointed to the map. "He worked here on the other side of the bay and lived here. Again, we have no explanation regarding why he was even in the city. His wife and co-workers said that he didn't have any plans that they knew of to be there. Just like with Mr. Falco, we don't know where the crime scene is. We have nothing. We have no idea where his murder took place, and there doesn't seem to be any connection between the two victims."

"Besides the killer, that is," Logan corrected. "So far, he's the only link to these two victims. And, it appears he's the only link to where they were found. There are no suspects in this case. And right now, we are basically spinning our wheels just as the police are. But, we still want to back track and interview the same people they did to see if you can pick up anything that could shed some light on this case."

"We have arranged to speak to Mr. Falco and Mr. Dukes' co-workers tomorrow. Were you able to get your morning cleared for tomorrow?" Ethan asked.

"Yes. I am free until at least two," I answered. "I can just work a little later tomorrow, or bring some work home."

"Great," Logan said sounding pleased. "We'd like to go ahead and interview Mr. Dukes' widow tonight if you are up to it. It would mean less to do by two tomorrow."

"That's fine," I replied.

"I can have Maya confirm with Mrs. Dukes that we can meet with her this evening." Logan said. "Are you hungry now, or can you wait until after we interview Mrs. Dukes?"

"No, I'm good. Let's go."

Chapter 4

Mrs. Dukes was expecting us and met us at the door. She was a slim, red headed woman who had clearly had better days. Though grief showed clearly on her face, she was still well groomed with her hair in a stylish shoulder length bob. She wore a printed baby doll top with jeans. For a woman who had two children under ten, she looked great.

"Thank you so much for seeing us, Mrs. Dukes," Logan was saying as he took Mrs. Duke's hand in his in a comforting grasp.

"It's no problem," she said in her scratchy voice. It was clear that she was suffering and had done a lot of crying. "I just don't know what else I can tell you."

"You don't need to feel that you have to tell us anything that you didn't tell the other investigators," Ethan assured her sympathetically. "We just want to ask you some of the same questions they probably did. It's just easier to get a big picture if we hear the answers directly from you."

After we all introduced ourselves, she led us to a cozy dining room and gestured for us to take a seat.

"Can I get you something to drink?" she asked fidgeting with her fingers. I opened my senses, bracing for the emotional pain that I would feel emanating from her.

"No. Don't worry yourself. We are fine," Logan answered in that calming tone of his.

"I'd like a glass of water," I spoke up, sensing she just needed to keep busy. Both Ethan and Logan glanced at me and gave barely perceptible nods.

Mrs. Dukes jumped up to get me some water. While she was up, I thought it best to get her talking now, hoping she would be fine once she got started.

"Where are your kids?" I asked in what I hoped was a light tone. It worked. She smiled.

"They are with my parents," she said turning her sad smile on me. "I am staying with them. But, I needed to do some things around here, so I let them stay there. I've got tons of laundry to fold. If I don't get to it, we won't have any clothes to wear."

She let out a nervous little laugh after her last words. *I'm babbling,* she thought to herself.

"Don't let us interrupt," I said sincerely. "Would you like us to sit somewhere else where you can get your clothes folded and talk to us?"

Yes! I don't want to sit still, came her mental reply, but her face looked pensive. Of course, she didn't know I could read her thoughts. And, she was worried about being rude. I strove to put her at ease.

"Just tell us where you want us," I encouraged before she could decline out of politeness.

"Well, the family room would be best, if you really don't mind?" she said sounding unsure.

"We don't mind at all," Logan smiled, following my lead.

Once we settled in the family room, where Mrs. Dukes indeed had a pile of laundry waiting, Logan and Ethan were able to start their questions.

"Mrs. Dukes, do you know of any reason that your husband would be in or around the Tenderloin neighborhood?" Ethan asked.

"I don't really know one place from another in the city," Mrs. Dukes replied in confusion. "But, from what the other investigators said, it's not a good area. I have no idea why he would need to go there. But, he has to meet clients in the city sometimes, so he could have had a reason I didn't know about."

"Do you know of anyone your husband might have had a conflict with recently?" Logan asked.

"No. No one. I mean, I fussed at him about leaving his socks and underwear on the floor the morning before...," she trailed off and her face buckled. Her next words came out as a whisper, "before he died. That's the only conflict I'm aware of, if you can call it that. I just thought it was called being married."

Ethan handed her a handkerchief he seemed to pull out of nowhere. Those Alexanders were always prepared for anything, even a woman's tears.

"Mrs. Dukes, when was the last time you spoke to your husband?" Ethan asked gently.

"That same afternoon. He told me that he was going to be working late, which was nothing unusual. He did that from time to time," she answered, visibly pulling herself together.

It was becoming very clear to me that Mrs. Dukes knew nothing. Both Ethan and Logan must have been thinking the same thing, because they each discretely looked at me for confirmation to see if I was getting anything. I gave a barely perceptible shake of my head. The only thing I was getting from Mrs. Dukes was confusion and emotional despair.

"How often did your husband work late?" Logan asked.

"It varied. Sometimes it was once or twice a week. Other times it would be several months before he worked late again. It all depended on what projects he had going at the office," Mrs.

Duke said in a dull voice. She was clearly tired and trying to just get through our questions. Logan asked a few more questions and then wrapped things up.

"Thank you so much for your time, Mrs. Duke," Logan said and stood. Ethan and I automatically stood as well.

"It was no trouble," she said looking anxious. "Mr. Alexander, will you let me know if you find out what happened to my husband?"

"We certainly will," Logan reassured her and handed her his business card. "And if you think of anything else, please feel free to give me a call no matter how insignificant it seems."

"Thank you," she said with a watery but grateful smile.

I shut down my senses immediately. The poor woman was breaking my heart. And the intensity of her grief was almost debilitating for me. I was walking out to the car and had unconsciously wrapped my arms around myself. I was cold, though the temperature outside was pretty darn hot.

"You ok?" Ethan asked sliding an arm around my shoulders and looking down at me with worry.

"Just trying to shake off her grief," I said practically near tears myself.

"Usually I envy that little gift of yours to read the thoughts and feelings of others, but this isn't one of those times," Ethan said giving me a squeeze and opening the car door for me.

"What can we do, Lela?" Logan asked looking concerned.

"Nothing," I said offering a tight smile. "I'll be fine. Just give me a minute. Don't worry."

"Are you sure," Logan asked doubtfully.

"I'm sure," I nodded. "Getting me back to the ranch and feeding me will help a whole lot too."

"I take it you didn't get much from Mrs. Dukes?" Ethan asked.

"No. She doesn't know anything that would help us. She's just shell shocked and grieving."

"Well, she did give us some new information," Logan chimed in. "I'm just not sure what to do with it."

"Yea, but something tells me that if we can figure it out, we will be on our way to finding out what's going on here," Ethan said grimly. Turning to see my confused expression from the backseat, he began to explain. "According to Mrs. Dukes, Mr. Dukes told her that he was working late. According to the statements the police got from his co-workers, he left at his usual time of around six thirty in the evening. That makes me think that whatever happened to Mr. Dukes was not some random act of violence. He was up to something."

"Sounds like," I agreed. "Well, whatever it is, the wife didn't seem to know anything about it."

"Yea, which leads me to think another woman was involved," Logan mused wryly.

"I was thinking the same thing," Ethan nodded.

Chapter 5

Jordan met us at the door when we arrived back at the ranch.

"How did it go?" he asked scrutinizing my face.

"It went fine," I replied with what I hoped was a cheery smile. He didn't look convinced, but he didn't say anything more.

"Lela needs to eat," Logan stated.

"We're all in the dining hall already," Jordan said. "I was waiting for you guys to return."

"You didn't have to wait." I couldn't help my smile.

"I know I didn't, but I didn't want to eat without you," Jordan said giving me a heated grin back.

"Get a room," Ethan teased heading for the dining room. Jordan winked at me and led me into the dining hall.

Dinner at the Alexanders was always a raucous affair. There was always plenty of food and plenty of laughs. Daniela, Logan and Grace's two year old daughter, cautiously stayed near me. The last time I'd seen her, she'd accidently almost killed me.

Logan and Grace had two children, Daniela and Tyler. Daniela would soon be two and Tyler was soon to be four. Being half healer and half drainer, and never having been around normal people, no one in the family had known exactly what traits they had. Drainers and healers tended to keep to themselves. And, not knowing what their unpredictable offspring might do, it was normal for them to keep their children away from all regular humans until they learned to interact without giving themselves away. I had been the one exception, and Daniela had immediately become attracted to my life force. Not knowing what she was doing, only that she wanted it, she'd almost killed me within shouting distance from Jordan and Logan.

I suspected she was given strict instructions not to touch me, because we were being watched like a hawk. Jordan didn't leave my side. Normally, Jordan would hold his niece on his lap and carry her everywhere. This evening, however, he had declined to do so. I could see that Daniela was crestfallen over the loss of her uncle's attentions for the evening. Truth be told, I really didn't want her to touch me either, however, I felt she needed a chance to redeem herself. I made a mental note to give her a big hug before we left. She was still so remorseful. I knew she'd learned her lesson, even if I still wanted to stay away from her.

Tyler, on the other hand, was sitting on the other side of me touching me all he wanted. Jordan had explained to me that after my unfortunate incident with Daniela, Grace and Logan had consulted the nanny and done some experimentation on their own to find out their children's abilities. Usually the nanny handled such training. And, since the children never came in contact with normals like myself, Logan and Grace hadn't given it much thought. Turns out that both kids had the ability to drain and heal. However, Daniela's dominant trait was that of draining and Tyler's was that of healing.

After dinner, and the showing of my vacation pictures I'd promised, Jordan announced it was time for me to go home. He'd tried to make the announcement before I showed the pictures, but Grace wasn't having it.

"She's got to get up and go to work in the morning, Grace," Jordan had protested.

"You just want to get her to yourself. I don't hear Lela complaining," Grace responded with a knowing look at Jordan. She was having no mercy on him as she turned to me. "Lela, are you too tired to show us your vacation photos?"

"Not at all," I chuckled.

We all went into Logan's office and he pulled up the email I'd sent him. Once the online album came up, there were plenty of questions and laughs to go around. Knowing that Ethan and Daisy loved looking at my photos, I'd sent Logan an abbreviated album. I tried to choose the best of the best, otherwise I'd have been there all night.

"These are really great pictures," Grace said sounding impressed.

"I told you!" Daisy was saying. "Some of them should be blown up and stuck on a wall. They are amazing. Did you see the one of the coastline at sunset? It's stunning."

"It really is," Logan agreed.

"Logan, you are going to have to take me on a vacation," Grace demanded as Jordan and I were headed for the front door.

"The only time I get to travel is for business. I don't think we've been on a decent vacation since the kids were born."

Jordan chuckled as he pulled me out the door.

"Grace, Honey, we can go wherever you want," Logan was saying as Jordan pulled the door closed behind us. I had to laugh. Logan and Grace were just so cute together. Jordan opened the passenger side door of my car for me, and I happily got in. Jordan then climbed in the driver's seat, and I was content to close my eyes and rest my brain on the companionably quiet ride home. It had been a long day, and I was ready for it to end.

Chapter 6

When I'd arrived home, Blake had come out of his room to greet me. I could hear his television and saw that he was clearly dressed for bed. Jordan had quietly disappeared before Blake ever knew he was there.

"Hey. Long day?" Blake asked as he pulled me in for a brotherly hug.

"Yea. The Alexanders asked me to help them out on another case," I told him. "So, I went straight over there after work."

I had told my brother about my helping the Alexanders and my gift during the prior case. To my surprise, my brother had already been aware of my gift. He'd also been under the impression that I no longer possessed it. He still wasn't aware, however, that the Alexanders were something much more than just regular humans.

"Another case, huh?" he said, and I could see the flicker of mingled interest and concern in his eyes. He didn't like the idea of anyone else knowing about my gift for obvious and valid reason. However, he thankfully liked and somewhat trusted the Alexanders, even though neither of us was the very trusting kind.

"Yea," I shrugged.

"Well stay safe. I'm headed to bed," he said and headed back to his room. "Night."

"Night, Blake."

I made my way to my room only to find Jordan already there. I was never sure how he managed entering undetected, but I suppose I'd gotten used to expecting him. So after my chat with Blake, I wasn't surprised to find Jordan there.

"So, how did it really go today with Mrs. Dukes?" Jordan asked. "You looked a little upset when you came in."

"It was just really hard feeling all of her emotions," I replied, sliding onto my bed next to him. Just like every other night, he pulled me closer to him with a possessive hand or arm around me somewhere. He was propped on one elbow now looking down at me with the other arm draped across my belly.

It had taken Jordan quite some time to gain my trust and convince me to reluctantly agree to date him. But, I'd finally given in. And, so far so good. We were going on four weeks as a couple of sorts. Granted, I'd been on vacation for one of those weeks.

It wasn't that I didn't want to be with Jordan. It was more like I wanted to be with him too much. Everything about him drew me uncontrollably to him. He was gorgeous. He had the body of life. And, if I didn't keep control of myself, I'd probably just sit and stare mindless of the drool I was producing over his well-made, perfectly chiseled body along with that raven dark, slightly curly hair and those dark, fathomless eyes. Yea, his hotness factor was off the charts. But, in addition to all of that, he was so sweet, attentive, caring and just irresistible. He made me feel like he loved me more than it was possible for a man to love a woman. While I knew that was the type of fairytale love most women wanted, I wasn't one of them. Most of those women weren't realistic in my view. A man like that was, at best, a loyal, loving man who would still stop taking you out and spoiling you once the newness wore off in exchange for making you sit through sports shows at home while he sat around in his underwear. At worst, he was just a player and was hoping you were just dumb enough of a woman to fall for his act. I was pretty darn certain that Jordan was the loyal sincere kind, and that scared me even more. I was afraid of losing myself with Jordan. Another guy, I could guard my heart against. Jordan's persistent draw seemed to always keep me helplessly treading water to keep from drowning willingly into him.

"Ethan told me about the case file pictures," he said rubbing his thumb in circles along my side where his hand now rested. "That couldn't have been pleasant."

"It wasn't." Being pulled back to the time spent with the case files by his words, I shivered with revulsion as I recalled the grotesque photos. I looked up into Jordan's watchful eyes as he gazed down at me. "How do you guys deal with this ugly side of humanity day in and day out?"

"I guess we're just used to it," he shrugged and then dipped his head to give me a soft kiss. Before either of us could get overly enthusiastic I broke the kiss.

"So, when exactly is your brother going back to work?" Jordan asked trying to sound casual.

"Wow," I laughed. "Now you're trying to rush my brother back to work?"

"I was just asking," he grinned.

"I'm sure he'll go back whenever he's supposed to," I said smugly.

He gave me a calculated look before bending down and capturing my lips in a demanding kiss. And just like that, I was on fire. He teased and coaxed until I was almost begging. Then abruptly he pulled away and rolled onto his side. I opened my eyes and blinked at him in confusion.

"What are you doing?" I asked, narrowing my eyes at him.

"Stopping before you get too carried away," he said innocently. His smoldering eyes gave him away. He knew he was far too late to prevent me from getting carried away. Still, I gathered what was left of my self-control and rolled off the bed.

"I'm going to go take my shower," I announced trying not to sound or appear as turned on as I was. I was ready to rip both of our clothes off. However, of the two of us, I had more self-control. I was determined to use it. I grabbed my pajama bottoms and tank top and headed for the shower.

I closed the door of my bathroom without a backwards glance. Then, I turned on the spray of the shower to hot in order to let the water heat up while I stripped out of my clothes. Seconds later, I was adjusting the temperature and stepping into the warm spray. I probably should have been taking a cold shower, but I felt like my poor aroused body was being tortured enough. I grabbed my little scrubby just as I heard a light click. I turned to see Jordan, gloriously naked through the clear shower curtain. He'd closed the bathroom door behind him.

As a kid, I loved watching scary movies. As a result, I always had to have clear shower curtains. I'd watched too many shower scenes where the woman couldn't see who was coming before the killer knifed her in the shower. Clearly, seeing Jordan advance towards me in all of his perfected male glory was yet another reason to always use a clear shower curtain. It wasn't until he pulled the shower curtain aside and stepped in the shower with me that my brain began to function again. I realized this was probably not a good idea.

"Jordan, what are you doing?" I asked not sounding nearly as disapproving as I should.

"Shh. Blake might hear you," he said taking my scrubby from me and grabbing my body wash. He poured some body wash on the scrubby.

"Exactly! You can't be in here," I hissed as my eyes dropped to his hands and watched those strong hands lather *my* scrubby.

"Why not? I'm just taking a shower. It's not like your brother is going to come in here while you are in the shower. Well, unless he's wondering why you are in here talking to yourself," he said as he gently turned my back to him and then pulled me to him. Then he began rubbing my scrubby over my back. "Here let me help you."

"I'm quite capable of washing myself," I mumbled, but I didn't do anything to stop him. In all honesty, I was having a hard time remembering that I was supposed to be protesting.

"I know you are," he whispered huskily in my ear as he splayed one hand low on my belly and brought the scrubby around to glide lightly between my breasts as he watched over my shoulder. "But, I thought we'd both enjoy this better."

My breath hitched and a delicious heat began spreading low and deep inside me. My breasts where tingling and straining for his attention as he slowly and languidly brushed the scrubby over one and then the other with feather light strokes. The combination of his methodic stroking and the water sluicing over me had me choking back a whimper.

"Shhh," he murmured in my ear. "You have to be quiet."

The other hand on my belly made its way slowly down one hip and to my inner thigh. My legs widened of their own accord, but Jordan simply followed a continuous path from my hip to my inner thigh and back, teasing me mercilessly.

"Jordan," I said through gritted teeth, my forgotten protest turning into a demand.

He had the nerve to chuckle. "What, Lela? What do you want?"

"You know what I want," I growled turning partially in his arms to glare at him.

"What? This?" He said sliding his hand down and cupping me directly between my legs with his left hand as he cupped my right breast with his other hand. He covered my mouth with his to stifle my moan of pleasure. My hips involuntarily jerked against his hand seeking more, but Jordan was holding back on me. I whimpered again in frustration this time.

"Are you ready for me, Lela," he asked against my ear. I could hear the urgency building in his voice as his breathing picked up, and I could feel his breath coming against my neck.

"Yes," I panted out as he bit gently down on my shoulder. I was leaning all of my weight against him now, my own legs feeling like jelly.

"Tell me you want me," he demanded.

"Jordan," I gasped. He flipped me around, placing my back against the cool tile as he stepped to me pressing into me. I could feel his hardness pressing into my stomach as he slid two fingers inside me. My eyes closed and my head fell back against the tile as I arched into his hand. I bit down hard on my lip to prevent the cry of pleasure that shot through me from escaping. Jordan covered my mouth with his as he began to slowly tease and torture me with his fingers. He kept brushing that most sensitive spot and moving away as if he were purposely trying to drive me out of my mind. I was clutching at him, gasping, whimpering and finally pinching him in overwhelming frustration.

"Jordan," I panted tearing my mouth from his.

"Tell me you want me, Lela," he commanded sliding two fingers deep inside me as he pressed down on my clit with his thumb. My body jerked violently against him.

"I want you, Jordan, now," I cried desperately.

Jordan slid both hands swiftly under me and lifted me. I wrapped my legs around him just as he slid deep inside me, pressing his weight against me and pinning me to the wall. His mouth came down hard on mine and his tongue slipped into my mouth, stifling my passionate cries. He didn't move for a long moment as he plundered my mouth with his. After an immeasurable amount of time he gently began to move, rocking gently at first against me.

I was lost. Jordan hadn't touched me in over a week and I was out of control for him. I moved against him trying to get even closer. How I ever thought I could have any self-control around him was a mystery. At my insistent squirming against him, his self-restraint began to unravel. What started out slow and sweet was rapidly becoming hard and fast. I arched into him as he began setting a hard pace. He kept his mouth over mine, swallowing all of my moans and whimpers and stifling a few groans of his own, until I finally came apart in his arms. For once, Jordan was right behind me unable to hold back his own release any longer.

I found myself unable to meet his eyes, afraid of what I might see there as our heart rates returned to normal. For all my mental control and my ability to control my environment, my body had clearly switched teams. And, Jordan was its master. As glorious as our lovemaking had been physically, the ease with which he broke my self-control had uneasiness churning inside me. I knew Jordan had total control of me when it came to my body. Even worse, I was starting to fear that he might know it too. At the moment, I wouldn't waste energy fighting it. I'd need all the energy I could muster to make sure physical control was the only thing I completely lost over myself with him.

He released me slowly and stepped out of the shower to hand me a towel. I could feel him watching me closely and was thankful he didn't push. He didn't say anything and didn't touch me, as if he knew I needed just a little distance at the moment to regain some self-possession.

I wrapped the towel tightly around myself as he made his way out of the bathroom. I let out a deep breath I hadn't been aware I was holding. What a coward I was. But, what had just happened was way too intense, too raw. I dried myself off, slathered on some body lotion, and put my clothes on.

When I stepped out of the bathroom the lights were already out. Again, the fraidy-cat in me was grateful that I wouldn't have to face Jordan just now, though he could probably see my face quite clearly with his super human vision. I climbed into bed next to him without a word.

"Night," he whispered in my ear as he settled beside me sliding an arm across my middle.

"Night," I whispered back.

A few short minutes later, I could feel his even breathing against my neck. He was asleep. I was not so lucky. I didn't finally get to sleep until the wee hours of the morning.

Chapter 7

The next morning I woke to find Jordan hovering over me looking very serious. Belatedly, I realized he was gently shaking me.

"Lela, sweetheart, wake up," he said gently.

I sat up abruptly, his concern getting through to me.

"What's wrong?" I asked blinking rapidly to try and get the sleep out of my eyes.

"Another body has been found. Grace is already there. It's a woman this time."

I was wide awake now. I hurried out of bed and got dressed. It was a little after six in the morning and it didn't sound like Blake was up yet.

"We can grab you some coffee on the way. I didn't want to wake Blake up making coffee for you," Jordan said confirming my assumption. Completely dressed now, I ran to the bathroom, combed my hair, pulled it back into one of my trusty ponytails, brushed my teeth and washed my face. Then we headed out the door.

Twenty minutes later, Jordan and I arrived at the crime scene.

"Do you want to stay in the car?" Jordan asked with a frown of concern creasing his brow. "Logan said that it wasn't brutal, but I don't really know what we are going to find here."

"Don't I *have* to stay here?" I asked. "I mean, there's crime scene tape everywhere. They probably won't let me in."

"You're part of Alexander Security and Investigation, Lela. They'll let you in." Jordan gave me an amused smile before his serious look returned.

"Yea, about that. How exactly did you guys get on this case?" I asked. I knew they worked directly with law enforcement at times, but I wasn't sure how that worked.

"There are several healers and drainers strategically placed in our local law enforcement. Whenever they catch a case like this one, where they know drainers are involved, they usually call us in as consultants to do the investigating that *they* really can't without giving themselves away to the normals."

"The normals?" I cocked an eyebrow.

"Yea," he smiled playfully. "You know. Like you."

"Uh huh." I gave him a mock glare.

"If there are any normals on the case, they often can't figure out what happened. In this case, like the dogs, it appears that the woman just died for no apparent reason. Once the coroner's office checks, that's most likely what the conclusion will be. However, since our contacts were already aware we were dealing with a case where dogs are being drained this way, and men are being brutally drained, Logan got a call this morning informing him of this case. That way, we can get a look at the crime scene and start our investigation right away. Apparently the first officer on the scene is a drainer and recognized the scent of a drainer and the cause of death."

"I see," I said for lack of anything better to say.

"So, do you want to stay in the car?"

"No. I'll come with you," I said reaching for the door handle. I wasn't keen on the idea of seeing a dead body. But, if I was going to be part of the investigation team, I guessed I had better do whatever everyone else was doing. Who knows? Maybe I would learn something that would help me do my job more efficiently. As long as this victim didn't look like the other two victims in those case file photos, I could probably deal with it.

"Hey, Jordan," the officer guarding the crime scene called out as we approached. "How's it going?"

"Not too bad, Smitty. How are you?" he called back as he lifted the tape for me to pass under and then ducked under after me.

"Eh, you know. Same old, same old," Smitty replied with a shrug and then turned his gaze to me. "New recruit?"

"Yea, she's with me," came Jordan's easy reply. Jordan continued walking, and I followed him into an old, rundown apartment building in a very scary part of the city I'd never been in. Walking down the darkened hallway, I couldn't help but notice the building was in sad shape and needed a good cleaning and some repairs. Once in the actual apartment, however, the cleanliness level increased dramatically. The apartment was old, but someone obviously took the time to keep things in good repair and clean in here. Everything was neat and tidy, if not a bit old and warn. It was a small two roomed apartment. The living and kitchen area could be cordoned off from a nook with a bed in it with sliding wooden doors. I supposed there had to be a bathroom somewhere, but I didn't see one.

The crowd around the bed turned to observe us new comers, and I finally got a glimpse of the lump in the small bed. There was nothing visible but a serene face framed by long dark hair. The woman looked as if she were huddled under the covers sleeping quite peacefully. She looked to be quite young, though there were tell-tell signs of a short life lived hard.

"Lela," Grace said coming over to my side. "You didn't have to come in here. Why didn't Jordan leave you in the car?"

"I wanted to come in," I assured her. This area was scarier than seeing a dead body. No way did I want to sit outside in a car by myself in this neighborhood. Grace looked doubtful but didn't speak. Jordan moved closer to the bed, and I followed staying a few steps behind him.

"Dr. Cole was just telling me that, so far she doesn't see any obvious cause of death. There doesn't seem to be any sign of a struggle or fight either," Grace informed Jordan and myself.

"I'll know more once I do a tox screening and a few other tests. From her liver temp, I'd say she died within the last six hours," Dr. Cole announced in a tired but friendly voice. "I guess for her line of work, if she died this peacefully then it's a blessing."

I gave Jordan a puzzled look just as he began to speak. "Do we have an ID on the victim?"

"According to the apartment manager, the lease holder is a Blanca McGrath, twenty-three years old," A young officer standing near the bed began reading from a notepad. "And, according to the photo ID found in her wallet, that's who our victim is."

"Thanks, Michelle," Jordan replied giving the young officer one of his devastating smiles. She blushed. Poor girl. I knew just how she felt being on the receiving end of one of his smiles.

"Jordan, I am going to go with Dr. Cole and the body back to the morgue," Grace advised. "Will you look around here with Michelle to see if you can find anything that might help us here?"

"Sure thing," Jordan answered.

"I really haven't found anything," Michelle shrugged. "But, considering there doesn't actually seem to be a crime committed here, I don't know what to look for. On initial inspection we didn't find any obvious bodily fluids on the sheets, so it doesn't look like she brought her clients here. Once the body is removed, we'll have a team come in and check out the bed and mattress though. Other than that, I don't know what else we can do."

My eyes widened with understanding, and I saw Jordan smirk as he saw the understanding dawning on my face. Blanca was a prostitute.

"Have you found any next of kin?" Jordan asked, walking slowly around the room as if looking for something.

"Not so far. We found a cell phone, but there were only incoming calls from one person. We're having the number tracked down," Michelle answered in the professional tone she'd managed to achieve once she'd started talking about the case.

After a few more moments of poking around, Jordan was ready to leave. I was happy to leave with him. Dr. Cole was getting ready to have the body removed, and I didn't want to stick around to watch. From there we headed directly to Mr. Drakes office to interview his co-workers. After several more hours of interviewing the co-workers of Mr. Drakes and Mr. Falco, we made our way back to the Alexander Ranch.

Chapter 8

"We didn't get any new information from Mr. Falco's or Mr. Dukes' co-workers," Jordan was saying. We were all assembled in the Alexander conference room for a debriefing of everything each of us had found.

"Lela, you didn't pick anything useful up?" Logan asked.

"Nothing other than Mr. Dukes' personal assistant mentally theorizing that he was probably caught with someone else's wife and the husband killed him. I remembered you and Ethan mentioning that you thought another woman might be involved. The personal assistants thoughts might add credence to your theory, but I'm not sure how that helps. She didn't seem to know for sure, or have any information on who he might be having this theorized affair with."

"And yes. I did ask her if she thought he might have been having a relationship outside of his marriage," Jordan added before Logan could ask. "I asked all of the standard questions."

"And?" Logan looked expectant.

"She simply said that she wouldn't have been surprised. But, she was unaware of who it could be if he was," Jordan answered.

"And, like I said, she didn't have any thoughts I could read that would indicate she knew more than what she was saying," I chimed in. "She apparently had heard him telling his wife he would be working late on several occasions when she knew for a fact he wasn't working late. Other than that, she didn't have any other thoughts about it."

"Well, Jordan and I confirmed that the scent of the drainer who killed the dogs was the same as that of the person who killed Ms. McGrath," Grace added. "So it would seem our killer of dogs is escalating as we feared. Although this is highly unusual. As far as I could tell, there was no sign of sexual contact in the case of Ms. McGrath and the drainer. That's unusual in these cases, even for someone who wasn't brutally drained. And the way we found her suggests that she was simply drained in her sleep. I've never seen a case like this. I'm not sure what to think."

I wanted to ask why that was unusual, but everyone else obviously understood. I was reluctant to publicly show my ignorance. I understood that drainers needed to occasionally take some of the life force of living things to survive. And Logan and Jordan did this regularly with the animals on the farm. They'd pet the dogs or cats, or ride the horses and drain minute bits of their life force. From what I could tell, the animals didn't seem to be any worse for wear. In fact, they were healthier than most. Jordan had explained that this was because whenever a life force was touched regularly and small amounts drained, it actually boosted the immune, respiratory, muscular and vascular systems. From what I could tell, it generally increased the overall health of the animal. He had also explained that the human life force was much more tempting to drainers. They could easily become addicted to it and kill someone, rather than take just what they needed. But, that didn't explain why our victim simply being drained in her sleep was so unusual. I decided to ask Jordan about it later.

"What about Elliot Falco? Did you get anything remotely interesting on him?" Daisy asked.

"No. Nothing. He worked long hours and was single as far as anyone knew," Jordan answered. "He went out with some of his co-workers from time to time, and picked up a girl from time to time at a bar or club. But, from what Lela was able to get, that was normal for them. They worked long hours, are young, and have a lot of cash. When they did get down time, they wanted to have some no strings attached fun."

"We still don't have a crime scene for him either," Ethan chimed in. "Without that, we don't have much to go on."

"It looks like we may have two unrelated drainer cases, folks," Logan said. "We've been asked to consult on both, so we will have to interact with law enforcement. You know what that means. Be careful around the normals. This isn't something that we can delegate to our normals. I'll try and give them whatever assignments I can, but the majority of the footwork is going to fall to us. They just can't find the stuff we are looking for. Besides, the local police are pretty much handling all of the normal stuff anyway. So, that's it for now."

With that, Logan ended the meeting. I had to get some work done so, after saying my goodbyes, I headed for the door.

"I have some work to do, and I don't know what time I'll be finished. I'll come by after," Jordan said walking me to my car.

"No. My brother texted me. He'll be flying out tomorrow and wants to get together tonight. I won't be home," I said.

"He had you for a week," Jordan said sounding incredulous.

"Well, Daisy is going to hang out with us too. Maybe even Ethan. Maybe you should join us," I suggested.

"What time?"

"About five o'clock."

"I can't. I won't be done by then." He shook his head. "I'll just come by when I get done."

"No, Jordan," I insisted and lowered my voice. "I'm sleeping alone tonight."

"But, -"

"No!" I hissed cutting him off. I'd decided after my complete and utter failure to put the brakes on last night that I would have to establish some boundaries. It was one thing for me to agree to give this whole relationship thing a try, but Jordan was practically moving in. The only time he hadn't slept in my bed since we decided to give this thing a try was the time I had been on vacation. Despite my uncontrollable attraction to him and his body, I was starting to feel uncomfortable. A look of resignation slid over his face, hiding his previous look of protest. It was as though he knew exactly what I was thinking.

"Ok, then," he agreed tightly. "Will you at least give me a text when you get in so I know you made it home safely?"

"Daisy and Ethan will be there. I'll be safe," I stated.

"Humor me."

"Fine. I will text you when I get in," I acquiesced.

Chapter 9

Daisy and I were sitting on the sofa talking after our dinner with Blake. Ethan had gotten caught up in whatever Jordan was working on, so it ended up being just me, Daisy, and Blake for dinner. Blake hadn't minded. We'd had a wonderful dinner, a few drinks, and a wonderful conversation. Blake and Daisy had flirted with each other outrageously. When we'd arrived home, Blake had headed straight for the shower. We both seemed to have to bathe before bed. Just the way we were raised, I guess.

"Thanks for such a wonderful dinner with two beautiful ladies," Blake had said once we were home. "Unfortunately I've got an early flight. I've got to get packed and get to bed. If you're still here when I'm done, I'll come out to say goodnight, Daisy."

"I'll be here waiting," Daisy said sending him a smoldering glance. I rolled my eyes.

"Ok, let me remind you," I gestured to Blake and then turned my glance to Daisy, "and inform you of the rules. You do not date the friends of your siblings or close relatives."

"Why not?" Daisy asked.

"Because. If things don't work out then you could ruin a friendship. Too messy. You wouldn't date Ethan or Jordan's best friend, right?" I asked just to make a point. I went on before she could answer. "And, you wouldn't want them dating your best friend."

"But, Jordan *is* dating my best friend," Daisy said sounding puzzled.

"Well…, but…that's," I sputtered, caught off guard by her simply stated words, "different."

"How's that different exactly?" Blake asked enjoying my flustered moment.

"Well, I met Jordan first for one thing. And, you know exactly why it's different, Blake Charles," I finished in a rush of agitated words.

"Well, we aren't dating anyway, so…" Daisy trailed off making a questioning gesture. I noticed she at least had the decency to look a little embarrassed. And, she couldn't seem to look at Blake at the moment.

"I'm headed for the shower," Blake chuckled as he turned and headed towards the hall and his room. "See you ladies in a few."

Now that Daisy and I were alone for a minute, I was able to ask the question I'd been wanting to ask since we left the meeting at the ranch.

"Daisy?"

"Hm?

"Why is this case of the drainer draining that woman so unusual? I understand how it works. Touching the life force of a 'normal,' as Logan put it, can be addicting. And, it sounds like it was for whomever drained Blanca McGrath. What's so unusual about that?" I asked. For the life of me, I had not been able to figure it out.

"Well, we never see cases where someone is drained so peacefully without showing signs of sexual contact. Some are brutal, but some are not. For those that aren't, it's usually because they were seduced and drained. The draining is part of some enhanced sexual experience from what I understand."

I vaguely remembered Jordan saying something along those lines when we'd first met. I guess I hadn't quite understood what he was talking about then.

"Well, what if the drainer was another woman who wasn't gay? She wouldn't have been attracted to another woman sexually," I frowned.

"She'd have most likely drained a man. Usually when we find men peacefully drained this way, it's because they were drained by a woman," she answered.

"Oh," I said, processing this information.

"Also, there was no attempt to hide the body," Daisy continued and then frowned in thought. "That may or may not be significant. If no one saw the drainer with this woman, then maybe it was safer to allow the body to be found there rather than risk being caught trying to move the body."

I made a non-committal sound.

"I heard you saw a dead body today for the first time. Did it freak you out?" Daisy asked.

"No. Not really," I replied thoughtfully. "She just looked like she was sleeping. If I think about it too much it might creep me out, but I just didn't think about it."

"Yea, I heard she looked peaceful. I still don't like the gruesome ones," she shuddered.

"How do you stand it?" I asked remembering my reaction to the photos of the dead men.

"It's just one of those parts of the job you have to do. Mostly though, Grace does it since she is the doctor," she shrugged. "She and the guys don't mind it so much. I only do it if she's not around and I have to."

Blake came out and said his goodbyes to Daisy, and she left soon after.

"Hey Brat," Blake said using his nickname for me and giving me a hug. "I really had a great time on vacation with you. It was like old times when all of us were together with Mom and Dad and we went on vacations."

"Those were good times," I agreed. Vacations with my family had always been wonderful. Though we really didn't stay in contact with our parents anymore if we could help it, I couldn't deny the good times. Due to major emotional blackmail and manipulation, my siblings and I tried to stay away for our own sanity.

"Speaking of family, Aila called today. She wants to bring the kids down to see us since she knew we were back from vacation. I told her that I could be back this Saturday, but I'd be flying out again on Sunday."

Aila was our older sister. She lived about two hours away with her husband and children. They lead busy lives and didn't make it down much to visit. Blake and I were workaholics so we didn't make it her way to visit often either. As a result, we didn't see them often. But when we all did finally connect, we always had fun.

"Sounds good. I'll be here," I said.

"Well, I'm going to pack a few things and then head to bed," Blake said with a yawn.

"Yea, I'm going to take a shower and head to bed myself," I said. "I'll text Aila also and let her know I'll be around. Can't wait to see the kids. Is Nigel coming?"

Nigel was Aila's husband.

"No. He's going out of town for a fishing thing with some friends. Of course, Aila and the kids would rather be doing anything but fishing. So, they decided to come and spend the weekend with us."

"Sounds like a plan."

I headed off to my own room to take my shower. Luckily, our house had two master bedroom suites, though Blake's was bigger than mine. Still, I had my own bathroom. It was just right for me.

Once I'd showered and climbed into bed, I sent my sister a message telling her I was looking forward to her visit. She replied quickly saying she was too. She hadn't told the kids yet though.

She didn't want them driving her crazy until the weekend. She warned me not to mention it if they called. I promised my lips were sealed.

After my texted conversation with Aila, I sent one off to Jordan telling him I was home. He replied that he knew since Daisy was home and had already told him. He followed that text with one asking if I wanted him to come over. I laughed to myself and told him no. He sent me a sad face back. I sent a final message saying I'd see him tomorrow and goodnight. Then, I slid under my covers.

Chapter 10

The next morning I'd barely gotten into the office when Ethan was ringing my phone.

"Hey Ethan. What's happened now?" I asked knowing something had to be wrong for Ethan to be calling me so early.

"Good morning to you too," he said sounding chipper. "Just wanted to let you know we got another dead body. Logan's going to want you filled in after they do the preliminaries."

Nothing riled Ethan. Apparently not even dead bodies.

"I just got here, Ethan. I can't leave now."

"Calm down," Ethan said in his unruffled voice. "We don't need you right now. Just head over when you get off work. We are all over the place right now anyway. We should all be back at the ranch, or some of us will, by about three."

"I can probably get there by 4:30," I estimated.

"That should be fine. I'll let Logan know. We should have more to go on by then. We don't have any witnesses, so we really don't have anyone to interview."

"Was it another woman or a man?" I asked.

"It was a man. And, he was brutally drained just like the others. Coroner says the man had a massive heart attack, but Grace could tell it was caused by the draining."

I shuttered and was grateful I didn't have to look at that body.

"Ok, I'll see you guys around four thirty at A.R.," I sighed.

"A.R.?" Ethan questioned, sounding puzzled.

"Yea. You know. Alexander Ranch. A.R.," I chuckled.

"Nice," Ethan replied and I could hear his grin. "See you back at A.R."

"Bye," I said and hung up. I tried to focus on my work, but it was a challenge. Who went to go talk about dead bodies after they got off work? Apparently I did.

When I got to the ranch at the designated time of four thirty, Beto and Shane were the only one's there to greet me. Beto worked for the Alexanders. He was one of the first people I met when I initially fell under the protection of the Alexanders. Kevin, another drainer, was trying to kill me at the time. Shane was my sparring partner. He also worked for the Alexanders, but more as an independent contractor or something. He wasn't exactly a regular member of the staff. He was, however, the guy I'd been caught kissing by Jordan before Jordan and I had decided to give in to our mutual attraction. Well, if I'm being honest, I was the only one who had been resisting the attraction between Jordan and myself by then.

Initially, I'd told Jordan that I didn't want to be anything more than friends in my futile attempt to resist him. I'd even thought of allowing Shane, who was delectable in his own right, to take my mind off of Jordan. That was until Jordan walked in on us lip locked after a six week absence. We'd all ended up working together on the last case and rescuing a kidnap victim. I hadn't seen Shane since. Not because we were avoiding each other. Life had just gotten busy, and I'd left for vacation.

"Hey, Lela," Beto said giving me a hug. "Heard you were soaking up some sun in Mexico. How was it?"

"It was very relaxing," I answered wistfully remembering just how relaxing it was. There were certainly no dead bodies and lots of free time. Between my regular job and working with the Alexanders, I was going to need another vacation real soon.

"Hi, Lela. It's really good to see you," Shane said more formally than usual. He made no move to come closer, or give me a hug, in the easy way he always had before.

"It's good to see you too, Shane," I said closing the distance between us and giving him a quick hug. He placed one hand on my waist, but made no other move to embrace me. I stepped back awkwardly. "Where is everyone?"

"They are on their way," Beto answered. "There was another dead body."

"Another one?" I squeaked and whirled around. "You mean besides the one they found this morning?"

"Yes. It was a woman this time," Beto replied. "They should be here any minute. We can head to the conference room."

Beto and Shane turned to walk into the conference room, but I reached out and touched Shane's arm to stop him. "Can I speak to you?"

"Sure," he said with only curiosity in his gaze. "What's up?"

I gestured outside, not quite sure that going outside would give us any more privacy from Beto's drainer super human hearing. I turned and walked out onto the front porch and Shane followed.

"Are we good?" I asked searching his face.

His eyes widened in surprise. "Of course. Why are you asking that?"

"Well, you didn't greet me like you normally do. And, I almost felt like you didn't want me to hug you."

He cocked his head to the side and gave me a speculative grin, "You didn't read my thoughts, or mind, or whatever it is you do?"

68

I sighed with patience. I'd forgotten he and Beto had been made aware of my little gift during our last case together, but we'd never talked about it since I hadn't actually seen Shane since. "No. Of course not. I don't just go around listening to people's thoughts. That's a rude invasion of privacy."

"Are you kidding me? If I had your gift, I would know what everyone was thinking all of the time."

"No you wouldn't. Trust me. Most of what people think, you don't want to know," I assured him. "Besides, do you really want me in your head listening to all of your random thoughts?"

He frowned and then looked at me suspiciously, "Absolutely not."

"So then, tell me. What's going on?"

"Well, the reason I didn't want to hug you was because I didn't want Jordan to smell me on you, not even a little bit."

"And?" I asked feeling there was more to it.

He frowned again. "Are you sure you aren't reading my mind and just making me say what I'm thinking."

"I'm not reading your mind, Shane," I said rolling my eyes at his suspicion. "I just feel like there is more to it than that."

"I haven't heard from you much since Jordan walked in on us kissing," he grimaced. "You didn't confirm our usual sparring sessions the two weeks before you went on vacation, and I haven't heard from you since you've been back. I guess you could say, I don't know exactly where we stand."

"I'm sorry, Shane," I said reaching out and touching his arm. "I was just really busy with work and trying to get ready for my vacation. We are perfectly fine as far as I am concerned. And, don't worry about Jordan. He knows we are just friends. He's fine with it."

He looked at me doubtfully, "Don't be so sure of that, Lela. I don't want to do anything to cause any problems with you and Jordan, or me and Jordan."

"He knows that, and I do too," I said giving his arm a squeeze. His whole body stiffened and I released him automatically. Looking at his face I realized he was looking at the road leading up to the house from the main gate. I turned around to see Logan's car coming up the drive.

"So, are we on for next week's sparring session," I asked, recapturing his attention. "I'm sure Daisy will be up for it too. Maybe even Ethan."

"Sounds good," he said distractedly. "I'm going to head into the conference room. I'll see you inside."

I stood there watching him as he re-entered the house. Was he seriously concerned about Jordan? Jordan knew that Shane and I were just friends, right? It was one kiss. And Jordan and I hadn't even started, well, whatever this was we'd started back then.

The car doors opened and the Alexander clan was pouring from Logan's SUV en masse. They all greeted me as they reached me on the porch.

"Lela, I'm glad you're here. We need to postpone our meeting for a few hours," Logan announced.

"I'll just let the others know while you fill Lela in," Grace said heading for the house.

Logan nodded and continued. "The local authorities have rounded up some of the other working girls that knew our female victims. They are going to be interviewing them and I'd like you to sit in on the interviews. They're waiting for us to get there so they can get started."

"Ok," I agreed eagerly, happy to have something to do.

Logan, Jordan, and I headed down to Logan's SUV and piled in. Twenty minutes later I was sitting in an observation room listening to the thoughts of several woman as they were interviewed one at a time. It was a singularly vexing and unproductive experience. These women knew absolutely nothing. They were afraid, but weren't even sure what they were afraid of. From all the reports, our two female victims had died of an unknown cause. We couldn't even really call them victims since the rest of the world knew nothing about draining. They were officially just suspicious deaths.

We returned three hours later to the ranch.

"Let's all meet in the conference room and get started," Logan ordered as he entered the house. Jordan grabbed my arm, stopping me from following.

71

"Hey," Jordan said as he bent down to kiss me lightly on the mouth. We'd been the last two to enter the house.

"Hey," I smiled up at him and then we followed the others into the conference room.

"What were you and Shane talking about?" came Jordan's thought directly into my head. I looked at him sharply, but his face hadn't changed. He still looked very relaxed. Was Shane right? Would Jordan be jealous of us talking and spending time together? He didn't look Jealous. I was just about to open my senses and read him when he sent me another thought. Yes, I know. I almost broke my own rule. But, I needed to know.

"I was just curious."

"Shane and I were just discussing when we are going to pick up sparring again," I said out loud. I turned to Daisy and Ethan. "I'm thinking next week? You and Ethan interested?"

I didn't ask Jordan because he never sparred with us. He said he couldn't spar with me because he'd be too concerned about hurting me. He claimed that he wouldn't be able to concentrate.

"Sounds good to me," Daisy said enthusiastically as we walked along the table towards the back of the room.

"I'm in. Just let me know when," Ethan agreed.

"Everybody, take your seats," Logan ordered. We all sat down and Logan jumped right in.

"We have two new victims, people. Kenneth Hayes, a forty-five year old museum director, not married and no current girlfriend as far as his co-workers knew. He was killed by the same drainer that killed our other male victims. He was also found not far from where the other victims were left in their cars. So, if we know nothing else about this guy, we know he only seems to pick victims with their own cars. The police are going to notify and question his next of kin, but none of them live in the area." Logan turned to me and spoke his next words. "Since they aren't local, and as far as we know you can't read thoughts through telephone wires, we figured we'd let the police handle the next of kin aspect."

Logan winked at me and laughed quietly at his own little joke.

"Jordan and I worked the second victim's case," Grace continued, looking amused at her husband. "The call came in while we were all at Mr. Hayes' crime scene. So, Jordan and I left to check out the second victim. Again, everything is the same. There were no signs of struggle and no sexual contact with the body as far as we could tell. Colleen Markov, age twenty-five, just seemed to simply die in her sleep to the regular authorities. She was also a prostitute. She appears to have been an immigrant. We are having her looked into in order to find next of kin. Jordan and I determined it was also the same drainer who killed our first female victim Ms. McGrath and the dogs."

73

"This is nerve-racking," Ethan ground out in frustration. "I mean, we have bodies dropping like flies and absolutely no real leads on this."

"Actually, Jordan may have found something. Though, I'm not sure it will help a lot," Grace said.

All eyes turned to Jordan.

"Well, I'm not really sure what I found," Jordan began. "After doing the sniff test on Mr. Hayes, as Grace said, we immediately left to check out Ms. Markov's crime scene when the call came in. I immediately did the sniff test on Ms. Markov to determine if she was drained by the same drainer as the dogs and Ms. McGrath. However, the scents surrounding Mr. Hayes were still very strong in my memory and probably on my person."

He paused for a moment seeming to try and figure out how to explain his next words, or to figure out what, if anything, it meant.

"Well? Don't leave us hanging in suspense," Daisy said breaking the silence in the room with her impatient outburst.

"Well, I'm certain there was something similar about the two smells. Yet, they were two very different smells," Jordan finally said. "I don't know how to explain it. There was something in the nuances of the smells and scents of the drainer that killed Mr. Hayes that was also in the smells and scents of the drainer that killed Ms. Markov."

"But, what does that mean?" Beto asked looking totally perplexed.

"We don't really know what it means," Grace chimed in. "Jordan wants to do more sniff tests on the previous bodies, including those of the dogs if that's possible."

"I can arrange it," I agreed.

"The only theory I could come up with was a hormonal or some other sort of change maybe." Jordan contemplated aloud. "Not being a medical person I don't know if that's even possible."

"What do you mean hormonal?" Shane asked.

"Well, you know how animals can smell fear? It's the hormones that change the body chemistry to smell differently. Or, rather, it can be smelled along with the normal body chemistry. I know this is wild speculation," Jordan shrugged, "but maybe this person hates men. Maybe when they encounter their victim, they send out a different smell based on their hatred of men. Maybe they love dogs and women, so they emit a more than slightly different smell."

"But, wouldn't that simply be a slight change in the smell based on a hormonal release? It wouldn't mask the person's basic smell would it?" Shane asked.

"I agree with you," Jordan nodded at Shane. "That's why I said it was wild speculation. We all know the smell of fear, and I've never known it to mask a person's regular scent. I also have my doubts that other hormonal changes, such as whatever is emitted during feelings of rage, anger, compassion, or caring can change a person's basic smell that much regardless of how strong the emotion is. However, I am fairly certain that something about this person's basic smell is present in both sets of victims. So, maybe there is some explanation that could explain how their scent is changing drastically during the different types of killings."

"What about you, Grace? Did you pick up anything?" Daisy asked. All eyes turned to Grace.

"No. But the sense of smell of healers is not usually as keen to pick out different smells within a smell. Drainers are far better at that than we are," She answered, swiveling her chair around to face everyone at the table. She had been sitting close to the head of the table with Jordan and Logan.

"Really?" Shane ruminated thoughtfully.

"Yea, man," Beto smiled at Shane. "You didn't know that?"

"I didn't," Shane said shaking his head.

"This just gets stranger and stranger," Daisy murmured. I silently seconded that statement.

"Yes it does," Logan agreed. "We all have follow-up work to do. Jordan, I'll join you in your sniff tests. The rest of you know what you need to do. No drainer needs this much life force."

"They might if they aren't eating regular food," Grace said thoughtfully. "When drainers go rogue, or are alone and without food, they tend to need more life force. Eating food helps nourish their bodies in a more well-rounded way. But in the absence of food, they tend to use whatever energy source is available."

"That's only if we are dealing with two separate perpetrators," Beto said. "One still wouldn't need the amount of life force that would leave this many bodies, even if he wasn't eating."

"True," Grace said with a nod.

"The only thing we know for certain at this point is that we have one or two perpetrators on a serial killing spree, likely two. We need to get a handle on this, because it's already getting out of hand."

With that, the meeting was dismissed.

"Jordan, we need to get our information down to Maya and Rene so they can update the case files," Grace said to Jordan as she headed towards the door.

Jordan turned to me, but I spoke before he could.

"Go on," I said waving him on. "I'll meet you down there in a minute. I want to chat with Logan for a moment. That way, when I come down, you'll be done. I want to say hi to Rene and Maya also."

He nodded and followed Grace out the door. I headed over to Logan while everyone else filed out of the room.

"What did you want to talk to me about?" Logan asked.

"Logan, I'm not feeling very helpful here. I don't mind helping out but, so far, I'm feeling pretty useless."

Logan laughed without any real humor. "I think you just summed up the way we are all feeling right now. None of us are feeling very productive right now, Lela."

"You guys are doing more than I am. Jordan smelled something that gives you guys something small at least to work with," I said in frustration. "What have I given you? I don't have super sensitive smelling abilities or anything else. Are you sure you need me?"

Logan put a hand on my shoulder. "Yes. We need you, Lela. You have a very valuable gift to offer. Just because it's not helping now, doesn't mean it won't help later. Trust me, we all feel like we are spinning our wheels right now. The only difference is, we've done this enough to know we just have to work through it. Something will pop. We just have to keep digging. Ok?"

"Ok," I said skeptically. Logan smirked.

"I think Ethan is right. We've created a monster with you," he said and then cocked his head and gave me a speculative look. "Answer this. Would you rather be on the case spinning your wheels with us, or would you rather me take you off of the case."

"I want to be on the case," I said as if he'd asked a dumb question.

"Yep. We've created a monster alright," he laughed.

"I'm going to go say hi to Maya and Rene," I said turning away to hide my smile. I was slightly less frustrated. Logan's words did make me feel better. I heard him chuckle as I headed out the door.

"Hey, girlie!" Maya said cheerfully when I entered the office where she and Rene were talking to Jordan and Grace. "Where have you been? We haven't seen you in forever."

"Jordan keeps her locked up and all to himself as much as he can," Rene teased before I could say anything.

"That's not true," Jordan protested.

"It kind of is," Grace said sweetly. "Logan and I never get to see her unless she's on a case."

"I'm fine. And I've been around," I interjected before anyone else could say anything. "And, Grace, you work all of the time. Between the ranch cases and the hospital rounds, you're always busy. I rarely see you even when I am here if we aren't working a case."

"That's true too," she conceded.

"I think we should have a girl's night out," Rene announced. "Grace, you have to tell us when you have an evening off and we should all go out."

"Sounds good to me," Maya agreed.

"Actually, that does sound good," Grace approved. "Some dinner, dancing, and a few drinks. It's been ages. Count me in."

"Ok, that's my cue to leave," Jordan said in mock disgust. "Come on, Lela. Let's go before they corrupt you."

"Just let me know when, and I am there," I said as I followed Jordan to the door. "I'll let Daisy know too."

"So, you'll go out to dinner, dancing, and drinks with the girls but not with me?" Jordan asked lightly as we headed to my car.

"I go to dinner with you all the time," I said in my own defense. "And, you've never offered to take me out dancing or for drinks."

"Well, you don't really drink, so that would be interesting," he frowned. "As for dancing, we can do that anytime you want."

"I'm going to have to hold you to that," I smiled up at him.

We arrived at my car and Jordan pulled the door open for me.

"I have to finish up a few things around here," he said pulling me to him. "I won't be long. Blake left this morning right?"

"Why yes he did," I said feigning wide eyed innocence and then rubbed my nose against his. "I'll be home all by my lonesome."

"Not for long you won't."

Chapter 11

Jordan was true to his word. I'd barely gotten out of the shower when there was a knock on my door. Of course, since Jordan never knocked, I was a little surprised to hear someone knocking at the door. Then, my phone went off. I picked it up, looked at it, and saw that it was a text from Jordan saying he was at the front door and to let him in.

"This is new," I said pulling the door open and tying the belt on my plush bath robe. Jordan's eyes travelled from my head to my toes and back up again. Then his face lit with a wicked smile.

"Come here woman," he said and lifted me off my feet as he kicked the door closed behind him. I let out a surprised squeak and then laughed as I wrapped my arms around his neck. He leaned me gently against the wall and murmured against my mouth. "Wrap your legs around me."

"Jordan -," I began before he silenced me by pressing his mouth to mine. He slid his hands from my waist down to my thighs and pulled them up around his waist.

All thoughts of protest fled as Jordan used his body weight and one arm to pin me to the wall while his other hand travelled down and between us. When he touched me I was lost. Those magic fingers of his had me pulling him towards me and trying to get closer, rather than pulling away in minutes.

"See, you're already wet for me," he said sliding in deep.

I came apart against the wall, but Jordan, who also had super human stamina wasn't done with me yet. He stumbled his way to my room and maneuvered us onto the bed, where he began again at a slow, steady pace. Where the first time was fast and hurried, this time was slow and oh so sweet. This thing between us was growing into something that was bigger than us both. And, my inability to control it was beginning to freak me out. This slow, sweet lovemaking of Jordan's was more devastating than the first to my self-control. I could feel myself trying to hold something back, something of myself for me, when he finally pulled me to him ready for sleep.

"I never get enough of you," he whispered into my neck. "But, I better let you get some rest."

"I do have to go to work in the morning," I said sleepily. I felt too exposed to talk to him right now. And, I was hoping he wasn't going to get all touchy feely on me and start talking about us.

"That's the only thing saving you, sweetheart," he said feelingly. Then, he asked something totally unexpected. I had the feeling he knew how I was feeling. He wouldn't push me right now. "Before you pass out, I wanted to ask you what you were talking to Logan about."

"I just asked him if you guys really needed me." I gave a lazy shrug of the shoulder I wasn't lying on. "I don't feel like I'm much help on this case."

"Trust me. We are all feeling like we aren't much help on this case," he said wryly.

"That's what Logan said," I mumbled.

"It's true. It's really hard when there doesn't seem to be anywhere to go, anything to follow up on, or anything to do to help solve a case. It's damn frustrating." Jordan placed his hand on my abdomen and began making slow circles in that way he seemed to love. "But, all we can do is keep digging."

"Like I said, that's basically what Logan said too," I reiterated trying not to be effected by his methodical thumb. "Jordan, why do you do that?"

"Do what?"

"Rub on me like that," I said feeling too tired to become aroused again, yet noticing my body respond anyway. The knowledge that his simple touch had such an effect on me both excited me and raised every internal alarm I had. He was breaking down too many of my walls much too quickly, yet I was helpless to stop him. His finger stopped its circling.

"I'm sorry. I didn't realize I was," he said and then pulled me over onto my back to give me a quick kiss. "I just like touching you. And, I guess I know that my rubbing you like that turns you on. So, I like it even more."

"Yes, well, I need to sleep," I said trying and failing miserably to sound stern. This was ridiculous. Enjoying being with Jordan was one thing. Losing total control of my body to him was another. I could see him grin in the darkness thanks to the little light seeping through the window from the yard lamp.

"Sleep is overrated," he said sounding pleased with himself.

"You won't be saying that when I turn into a harpy from sleep deprivation," I warned.

Sometime later, after another of Jordan's marathon love making sessions, I finally drifted off to sleep.

Chapter 12

Friday, thankfully, was uneventful. There were no dead bodies and no dead animals. I'd gotten up that morning and taken a long, thorough shower. Just in case I ended up meeting up with any of the Alexanders today, I didn't want to have any lingering smells on me from my night with Jordan.

The first night we'd spent the night together making love, I had taken a quick shower before being rushed out the door by Jordan to go save a kidnap victim. I hadn't figured out why all of the extraction team we were working with were sniffing the air until after the fighting and rescuing. Apparently the scent of our lovemaking had still been very strong on me. I'd been mortified to find that I'd been a walking, or rather, smelling telegraph to everyone about our private business. I did not plan to suffer that embarrassment again by being a virtual scratch and sniff.

I worked a full day uninterrupted. Aila had called earlier to tell me that she and the kids were coming down that evening. She had to wait until the kids got out of school, but she would be at my house roughly around the time I got home. I was just shutting things down so I could leave a little early when my phone rang.

"Hey, Daisy," I said in greeting.

"Hey," came her perky voice through the phone. "What time are you heading home?"

"I was just about to do that now," I replied.

"Cool! Let's do something tonight. We haven't had a dead body in a whole twenty-four hours. And, while we aren't any closer to solving this thing, I can at least be grateful for that," she said with feeling. "Besides, I'm off duty tonight. I want to have some fun."

"Well, I can't really go out tonight. My sister is coming down tonight, and she's bringing my nephews with her," I said feeling torn. I loved hanging out with Daisy, and we really hadn't had a chance to hang out much over the last few weeks. "You're welcome to hang out with us. I don't really know what we're doing yet though."

"I would love to meet your sister," Daisy said enthusiastically. "Aila, right?"

"Yes and her two boys, Elliot and Vince."

"It sounds like fun," she said. "I'll meet you at your house."

"See you there."

I hung up, shut everything down, grabbed my purse and headed for home. I was excited to get to spend time with my sister and the kids. Blake would be home tomorrow and we would all spend Saturday together. I was ready for a family and fun filled weekend.

I arrived home to find Daisy *and* Jordan waiting for me. Jordan had parked on the street. I waved as I passed them and pulled into the driveway. Before I could turn the car off and get out, my sister pulled into the driveway next to me.

"Great. First Daisy insisted on coming with me, and now she's telling me your sister and her kids will be staying with you tonight," Jordan said softly as he opened my car door for me. "So much for having you to myself tonight."

I knew he was only kidding. He had a smile on his face and no trace of irritation.

"I heard that," Daisy said getting out the car.

"Of course you did," I said wrinkling my nose at her before turning back to Jordan. "You had me to yourself last night."

"Yea, and I wanted you to myself tonight too. Is two nights in a row too much to ask?" he said without any real heat.

"Can we talk about this later?" I hissed as my sister got out of her car.

"Yes. Can you please talk about it later? Getting nauseous over here," Daisy complained and then snickered.

"Hey, Aila!" I called out, pushing past Jordan and giving my sister a warm hug.

"Hi, Auntie," the boys said as they spilled out of the car and wrapped themselves around me. I bent down for a group hug.

"Hi, boys!" I said enthusiastically and gave them both a big squeeze. I squatted down to get closer to their eye level. "Look how big you are. I missed you."

"We missed you, too," they exclaimed in unison.

"Mommy says we get to stay all weekend with you and Uncle Blake," Elliot said excitedly. Elliot's real name was Nigel Elliot Lekas Jr. But, since we aren't big on juniors in our family, and my sister's husband, Nigel Sr., wouldn't heed our pleas to give the kid his own identity, we all called him by his middle name, Elliot.

"Yea, because Mommy wouldn't let us go fishing with Daddy. She said he'd be too busy fishing and talking, and wouldn't notice if one of us fell in. And if that happened, then she would have to kill him. She said she didn't feel like going to jail this weekend," Vince, the obviously more talkative one, babbled on freely.

"She did?" I said with exaggerated interest. I knew it irked Aila when he babbled on about her business, so I egged him on. What are aunties for?

"Uh huh. And then I started to cry, because I really wanted to go fishing. Daddy said-"

"Vince!" Aila said with a tight smile and steel in her voice. "Auntie Lela doesn't need a blow by blow. Thank you."

I laughed. "Oh, but he was just getting started."

"Yes. I know," she said sardonically. "And, you were going to encourage him."

I stood and turned to face everyone for introductions. "Aila, these are some friends of mine, Jordan and Daisy."

"Nice to meet you," Aila said with a friendly, albeit reserved smile.

"Nice to meet you too," Jordan and Daisy replied warmly. I didn't fail to see that the warmth that was so natural for the Alexander clan was not natural at all in my family. Aila's greeting was perfectly friendly. But, I saw me and my one reticence upon meeting people in her.

"And these are my two favorite nephews, Elliot and Vince," I said with a flourish.

"We are your only nephews," Vince giggled. Elliot tried on a pitying look and directed it at me.

"That's why you're my favorite nephews," I said pretending I was confused. This brought more giggles from my two fun loving nephews. Elliot couldn't even hold on to his big boy disgruntled look.

Jordan and Daisy ruled Friday night with the kids. Apparently they played a lot of video games because, while they let my nephews win, they clearly knew their way around Blake's games.

"You're friends seem really nice," Aila said as we watched them whoop and yell at the screen as they played some sort of team game.

"They *are* really nice people," I said feelingly with a gentle smile I could feel blooming on my face.

"Blake said they were," she said smiling now. Her smile turned sly as she said her next words. "He also called a few weeks ago to ask me if you'd mentioned Jordan to me."

"He did?" I tried not to show my surprise.

"Yea," she said, eyes glittering with mischief. "I told him you hadn't, which was the truth. Then he clammed up when I started asking him who this Jordan was and why would you have said anything to me about him. He just said he thought something might have been going on between you and changed the subject."

I glanced over at Daisy and Jordan knowing full well that they could hear every word Aila was saying, despite her speaking in low tones. Jordan had a smug expression on his face while Daisy's lips were twitching like she was holding back a laugh.

Both appeared to be concentrating a little too hard on the video game they were playing.

"Well?" Aila said giving me a little shove. "Do tell."

"Jordan and I are getting to know each other," I said uncomfortably. I could swear I heard a snort of laughter from the direction of the television.

"Girl, who are you talking to?" Aila said in a voice that clearly said she wasn't buying it. "I have been watching you guys all evening. And, from what I see, I'm pretty sure he's gotten to know you pretty damn well. I'm thinking there isn't an inch of you he hasn't met personally."

"Aila!" I hissed. Jordan choked and Daisy had a coughing fit that sounded a lot like a fit of laughter.

"What?" Aila said putting her hands up, palms facing the ceiling. "I don't blame you. He's gorgeous and seems really nice too. And, he is definitely into you."

"So, is that the real reason why you decided to come down to stay the weekend?" I asked trying to change the subject and put her on the defensive. "You thought you'd come and interrogate me?"

"No. It wasn't," she said giving me a look. "You know if I'd wanted to come and check him out, I would have just told you that was what I was coming to do."

And I knew she was telling the truth. That was one trait my siblings and I all shared. We did not beat around the bush or pull any punches. She started to open her mouth again, but I put my hand up to stop her.

"This topic is now closed."

She laughed. "Ok. Have it your way. I've seen all I needed to see anyway."

After the video game wars, we all sat down to watch a movie with the kids. We popped popcorn and all found comfortable spots on the sofa or armchairs. Jordan sat with Vince right up under him. Elliot was eight and had been sticking to Daisy like glue all night. I suspected that he, like his Uncle Blake, had a thing for Ms. Daisy.

"Ok, guys. The movie is over," Aila said to the boys in her mommy voice once the movie ended. "It's time for bed."

They groaned and whined.

"I don't want to hear it. Get moving," Aila ordered.

"Auntie, can I sleep with you?" Vince asked.

"Sure you can, sweetie face," I said patting his little shoulders as he hugged me. Out of the corner of my eye, I saw Jordan giving me a pained look.

"Me too?" asked Elliot.

"Uh, sure," I said with a little less enthusiasm. Maybe if I put them together on one side I wouldn't be rolled over, kicked, and pummeled all night. Elliot was a horrible sleeper. Then an idea came to me. "Why don't we have a slumber party in the living room?"

"Yea!" Elliot said.

"Then, Daisy and Jordan can stay and have a slumber party with us!" Vince said enthusiastically. "Jordan, don't you want to stay and have a slumber party?"

"I'd love to stay and have a slumber party," Jordan answered giving me a smoldering look that had me tingling all over and flushing with embarrassment.

"Oh, my," my sister said looking away with a smirk on her face and sounding amused.

This seemed to remind Jordan of where he was and with whom. "But, I have to go home tonight, unfortunately. I have to work tomorrow."

"What about you, Daisy?" Elliot asked hopefully.

"I can't stay for the slumber party, but how about I come back tomorrow?" She said ruffling his curly hair. Then, she turned to me. "What are you guys doing tomorrow?"

"I have no idea. Blake will be in early, and I don't know what he'll want to do," I answered shaking my head at my nephew. "Whatever it is, you're welcome to join us."

Chapter 13

If Daisy and Jordan ruled Friday evening with my nephews, then Daisy, Ethan and Blake ruled Saturday. Blake got home very early before anyone woke up. I'd stayed in the living room on a king sized air mattress with the boys, intending to sneak off to my own bed once they'd fallen asleep. I woke up the next morning with a foot up my nose and a knee in my back. As I tried to extricate myself from the tangle of children and covers, Elliot woke up. Hearing Blake moving around in the kitchen, he jumped up yelling "Uncle Blake," which woke up Vince.

"Uncle Blake, can we play video games today?" Elliot asked.

"Well, we could," Blake said pretending great thought. "But, I was thinking more along the lines of riding roller coasters."

"Roller coasters!" both boys yelled and then began bouncing around excitedly. And, that was how the day began. Aila and I hurriedly grabbed some much needed coffee. As we were getting ourselves ready, Daisy called to check in to see what we were doing and was as excited as the boys when she found out we were going to Six Flags. She told Ethan, and they both showed up on our doorstep in record time.

We spent the day riding roller coasters and eating junk food until the park closed. Aila and I ended up taking turns riding rollercoasters to make it even. The boys kept switching partners to ride the rides with. I couldn't help but notice that Blake and Elliot seemed to be switching with Daisy quite a lot. And, Ethan seemed to be switching between Vince and Aila. We were all exhausted once the park finally closed. Well, at least us normal folks were. Of course, Ethan and Daisy looked like they could do it all again. Seeing that we were all tired though, I noticed they tried not to appear quite so energetic.

The boys fell asleep on the way back home. They woke up once we got home, but Aila had them shower, eat, and head straight to bed. They tried to protest but were too tired to put up much of a fight. Blake and Daisy chatted for a while in the living room while Ethan spent way too much time trying to charm my sister.

Once Aila had the boys ready for bed, she announced that she was going to get herself ready for bed. Aila was leaving early the next morning and so was Blake. Daisy pulled herself away from Blake long enough to suggest to Ethan that they should be going.

"Two days and no dead bodies," Ethan said as I walked them out to their car. "I'm glad, but I don't think it's going to last."

"I don't either," Daisy agreed. "But, at least we had a fun day. I haven't had one of those in a while. Without any real leads on the case, there wasn't anything for us to do today. So, I'm trying to see it as a good thing."

"I guess I'm not the only one frustrated and feeling useless," I said seeing the frustration on their faces.

"Definitely not," Ethan said gravely. "Get inside. Enjoy your family now. Go spend some time with that ridiculously hot sister of yours."

"My ridiculously hot sister is married," I said smacking Ethan on the arm.

"And I totally respect that," Ethan said solemnly. "Doesn't mean I can't enjoy the view."

"Come along, Ethan," Daisy said shaking her head.

"Oh, like you weren't drooling all over Blake all day," Ethan said giving Daisy a knowing look. "At least I'm up front about it. I'm trying to get invited to a family reunion. Clearly, the Charles family knows how to produce some gorgeous people."

"Goodbye, Ethan," I said laughing and shaking my head at him.

"I'll just take him home now," Daisy said pulling Ethan along.

I laughed again. If Ethan only knew. Yea, I did have a beautiful family. I'm not bragging, I'm just stating a fact. And half of them are just as crazy as they are beautiful. That was also a fact. I don't know of anyone in my family who hadn't been told they were beautiful in one way or another since they were born. We were constantly told that. However, sometimes beauty really is a curse. One thing I definitely can thank my mother for is that she never fell into the beauty trap. She would always say, "Beauty is as beauty does. You can be the most beautiful person in the world, but if you act ugly then you are ugly." I remember that making a lot of sense to me, because some of my cousins acted so weird just because they were "beautiful."

I remember one such cousin saying something about being beautiful, so she never had to work. Men were always willing to take care of her. And, outspoken just like the rest of us, my mother promptly told her that everybody in the damn family was beautiful and who cares. Another of her favorite lines was, "Get something in that empty head of yours, because beauty isn't going to get you very far. You need something between your ears."

Yea, Ethan would never go to a family reunion of mine. I would be embarrassed for him to find out just how many nuts where on my family tree.

After Ethan and Daisy were gone, I went back in and sat a few minutes with my siblings. We'd had a really great time.

"We have *got* to do this more often," Blake proclaimed as we were all heading to bed. The children were already asleep in Blake's bed. Blake could sleep through a hurricane, so he immediately agreed when they asked to sleep in his bed. Who knew what it was about sleeping with the adults as a kid? But, we all did it. If Mom or Dad went away on a business trip, we kids would pile in the bed and beg and plead to stay. Dad grumbled a lot, but he always gave in. Mom would let us all stay with her the first night. After that, she banned us and said she was going to sleep in peace with no snoring until Dad got back.

"I agree," Aila grinned a happy grin. "This was really fun. And, you guys seem to be having way too much fun down here without us. Since when did you guys start hanging out with friends and not being workaholics?"

"Lela, started it," Blake accused pointing at me. "She got mixed up with those Alexanders, and they just kind of rub off on you."

"Speaking of rubbing off, Ethan sure was charming you," I teased my sister.

She rolled her eyes, "Ethan is really cute and all. But, he's not my Nigel."

"Ethan is just a big flirt," I said relieved. "I was hoping you wouldn't take him seriously."

"Actually, he didn't flirt with me at all. He was just attentive," she said.

"Good. I didn't think he would, but I wasn't sure. He really is harmless though," I assured her.

"Don't worry little sister," she patted my arm. "He didn't do anything to offend me. He was nothing but a gentleman. They all seem like really nice people."

"They are," Blake confirmed.

"I did notice that Daisy was definitely flirting with you, Blake," Aila said giving Blake a knowing look.

"Oh, look at the time," Blake said with an exaggerated stretch. "Night."

"Wimp!" I yelled at him.

"I can't stand the heat, so I'm getting out of the kitchen," he called back as he disappeared around the corner heading towards his room. Aila and I chuckled, said our goodnights, and made our way to our own beds.

Chapter 14

Ethan was right. The cessation of murder victims didn't last. Aila, the kids, and Blake had gotten up early. Aila was heading home and Blake on business. After they left, I crept back into my bed to sleep in the rest of the morning only to be awakened by Jordan at eight thirty. I had been hoping to sleep until at least nine thirty and then lay around long after that. Instead, I woke to Jordan calling my name with a cup of coffee in his hand.

"Don't tell me," I groaned. "Another dead body."

"Two actually. Another man and another woman. The calls came in late last night. Logan and Grace worked one crime scene, and Ethan, Daisy and I went to the other crime scene. Everything is the same. We still don't know where the man was killed. This time the woman died on the street though. Still, there was no sign of struggle or sexual contact. Grace has her doubts about this girl being a prostitute too. She thinks she might just be a runaway."

"Then, if you guys have already been to the crime scenes, why are you waking me up?" I asked taking the coffee from his hands.

98

"Logan's calling a meeting, of course. We need to have a brainstorming meeting," Jordan said. "Get up. Get dressed. We gotta go."

I griped into my coffee as I took a sip.

"Oh," he said taking my coffee from me and kissing me sweetly on the mouth. "Good morning."

After dragging myself out of bed, hurrying through getting dressed, and being escorted to the ranch, I was back in the Alexanders' conference room.

"I know that we are all tired and frustrated with this case," Logan began. "And, I know we all know the facts of each case. But, we are going to look at them again. We are going to go through them one at a time and try to see if we are missing something."

He proceeded to talk about each victim, their background, employment, interview statements with their family or co-workers, and whatever other information he had. I have to say, I kept finding my mind wondering and I had to constantly force myself to pay attention. I kept staring at the map each time Logan put a sticky dot on the map where the victims were found. And, a thought process I wasn't sure about started to form in my head.

"We are pretty sure we are dealing with two killers here, since the timing of the last two sets of victims deaths were so close together. And, other than Jordan's smell test, we have no other evidence to the contrary. So we think that-"

"Logan," I said staring at the map and not realizing at first that I'd just interrupted him in mid-sentence. "I'm sorry. I didn't mean to interrupt."

"No. That's ok. What's on your mind?"

"Well, I'm looking at the map and all of the male victims were found not all that far from each other," I stated.

"Yes. We think that our murderer must have some ties here, or he's just chosen it as his dump site. It's not a very nice part of town," Logan explained.

"Ok, but the women were also found not very far apart," I pointed out.

"True. But, we think it's because that's the area where our perpetrator is doing his hunting, so to speak. Remember we interviewed some of the other working girls in that area? But you confirmed they didn't know anything."

"Yes, but what if the only tie to these men is the perpetrator. We could easily find out if the one that is killing the women is using that area as a hunting ground. Maybe we could do the same to see if the one killing the men is using the area he's dumping them as his hunting ground also."

"How could we easily find that out?" Beto asked in confusion. "We've been checking into their backgrounds, work, and personal lives. None of them have any ties to this area. We even put a few undercover agents in the area with the women, but we haven't gotten anything. The bodies still showed up despite the presence of the undercover agents. That's how they were found so quickly. When we use drainer or healer undercover agents, nothing happens at all."

"Ok, maybe not easy with your agents. Our perpetrator can scent your non-normal agents and get around your normal ones. But, you haven't tried using me," I said pointing out the obvious.

"Using you for what?" Jordan started and jerked his head around to look at me like I'd lost my mind. "No way are you going undercover."

"I don't think she's talking about going undercover, Jordan," Ethan said dryly. "Don't get your undies in a twist."

"Oh, you mean to do that little mind thingy you do?" Shane asked with a speculative grin.

"It could work," Beto said nodding thoughtfully now. "She was doing some crazy amazing stuff when we rescued Mr. Beck in that kidnapping case a few weeks back."

"What exactly are you suggesting," Logan asked cautiously.

"Well, if I go to the dump site, maybe I can read the minds around there and catch him in the act of hunting, dumping, or something. The other agents don't know where anything is taking place, and a drainer wouldn't have a hard time keeping his activities hidden from us normals," I explained.

"You aren't really so normal," Beto said.

"Yes, well. The drainer wouldn't know that. I could be sitting back in a car somewhere just filtering through thoughts. If I pick something up, I can just let you guys know."

"And since we'd already be there, we could handle it from there," Jordan said in an uncompromising voice as he glared at me.

"It could work," Daisy nodded thoughtfully.

"Well, it's worth a try," Beto said sounding hopeful. "It's not like we have a better plan."

"Let's set it up," Logan commanded cautiously excited. "We'll break up into two surveillance teams. One will go to the area where the women are working the streets. The other will go to the place the men are being dumped. This way we are still actively working on both cases. Maybe we'll keep someone alive."

"I'm going wherever she goes," Jordan said pointing to me.

"Jordan, Daisy, and Ethan will go with Lela," Logan continued smoothly over Jordan's brittle demand. "Grace and I will team up with Beto and Shane. That way each team has healers to help in the event that we have any victims."

"Saddle up and lets ride," Beto said rubbing his hands together.

"See, Lela. I told you that you were needed," Logan said with a huge smile on his face.

It was a very long night. It was now the beginning of September, and it was hot. Living near the bay, the breeze coming off the water often cooled things down in the evening even on hot days. However, tonight was one of those nights that was hot and sticky. We were having one of our heat waves that made for really hot days and hotter than usual nights. And, I was stuck in the car with Jordan, Daisy, and Ethan. I was randomly sifting through minds, which was enough to exhaust me by itself. The fact that it was past my bedtime only added to my fatigue. Nothing was happening. I was only privy to the sick and twisted thoughts of the perverted.

I had begun taking frequent mind breaks a few hours ago. We were sitting in Jordan's SUV with the windows down, but the air was too hot to really help. We'd all agreed though that sitting in a car, and keeping it running for the air conditioner, would be way too obvious. I was on one of my mind breaks when Jordan got a call. He spoke quietly into the phone and everyone seemed to relax with relief just as he was hanging up the phone. Of course, they could hear what was being said on the phone. I was the only one who couldn't.

"What?" I asked turning to Daisy, who was sitting in the back seat with me.

"Logan says nothing is happening in their area tonight either. He says we should pack it in and call it a night," she answered.

More like call it a morning, I thought to myself. It was after two in the morning. I had to get up and go to work Monday morning…well, this morning.

"Logan says we'll try again tomorrow night," Jordan added.

Chapter 15

By the time I got off of work on Monday, I was a zombie. I didn't go into the office until nine, since I hadn't gotten to bed until after three in the morning. I walked in the door at five in the evening, jumped in the shower, and fell into my bed. I didn't resurface again until Jordan rang my phone.

"I'm not home. Please leave a message," I mumbled sleepily into the phone.

"I had a feeling you'd be sleeping," Jordan chuckled. "Since we are short on time, I figured I'd better give you a wakeup call on the way in."

"I don't think I like you right now," I mumbled again with my face still half smashed in my pillow. "Besides, my plan didn't work. Nothing happened."

"Man, I love it when you talk dirty," Jordan teased. "You just don't know what it does to me to hear your sleepy voice. It's the sexiest thing I've ever heard."

I frowned. "Jordan?"

"Yea, Babe?"

You need your head checked."

He laughed and then I heard him talking to someone else before he came back to me. "Ok, we are all getting in the car now. Get dressed. We are on our way."

With that he hung up. I rolled over to look at the clock. It was nine o'clock. I groaned, dragged myself out of bed and pulled on some oversized terry cloth gym shorts and an oversized t-shirt, compliments of Blake's closet. It was hot, and it was going to stay hot, just like last night. If I had to be locked in a hot car, bored and tired, I might as well be comfortable.

"You still aren't ready?" Daisy said, wrinkling her nose at my attire when I opened the door to let them in. Daisy was the master of fashionably casual dressing. She wasn't always dolled up or dressed like she stepped out of the pages of a magazine, yet she always made the simple casual look appear effortless.

"Uh, yes..., yes, I am ready," I said firmly. "I just need to get my shoes on."

"You're going like that?" she asked in astonishment.

"What's wrong with this?" I said defensively. "It's not like I'm in my pajamas and slippers with curlers in my hair. I'm wearing shorts and a t-shirt."

"Yes, but that's barely acceptable for the gym," she said pointing at my ensemble.

"I don't know," Ethan said looking me over as he came in the door. "She's got this whole comfortable, lounge at home watching television look. It's kind of hot."

"Get your own girlfriend, Ethan," Jordan said shoving Ethan out of the way as he came in the door last. He bent down and gave me a kiss before pulling back to give me his own visual once over. "Though, Ethan does have a point. You look fine. Let's go."

I stuck my tongue out at Daisy, and grabbed my purse and keys.

"You do realize you are taking fashion advice from guys, right?" She said with a doubtful frown. "Just saying."

I ignored Daisy and we piled into the car.

"My plan didn't work," I said on a yawn. "Why are we going out again tonight?"

"Just because nothing happened last night doesn't mean it won't tonight," Ethan said from the front seat. "And, we are switching it up tonight. Logan and his team are going where we were last night. And, we are going where they were."

I sat back, closed my eyes, and listened to them chatter.

"You are really tired, huh?" Daisy said beside me.

"Yes," I said opening my eyes. "I only got about four hours of sleep last night."

"I keep forgetting you need more sleep than we do," Daisy said amused. "But, you seem to need more than most normals."

"Anything less than eight hours is not enough for more than a night or two," I said closing my eyes again. "I could never have been a doctor."

Daisy gave a delicate snort of laughter.

When we finally arrived, I roused myself into alertness. I started sifting through the minds of the people milling about. Again, it was the same as last night. The women where hot, bored and unenthusiastic, but trying not to show it. Some were scared and desperate. The men were simply repulsive. I sighed and continued to filter through the random minds around me.

After some time I flittered across one mind that caught my attention. It was different. There was a lot of anger and rage. It also had a healthy dose of disgust for the whole situation.

"There's someone here," Ethan said. I opened my eyes to see them all scenting the air.

"You smell it too?" Jordan said. "It's a drainer. Our drainer."

"Where?" I asked. Jordan rolled up the windows.

"I don't want him to hear us talking," he murmured in a low voice after the windows were rolled up. "I don't know where.

The faint breeze just blew his scent in our direction. Maybe we should get out and search."

"No," Daisy said doubtfully. "He can't be that far away. I picked his scent up too. Lela, have you picked up anything interesting."

"Yes," I said remembering the last mind I was listening to. "There was someone, well, observing."

"Observing what?" Jordan asked. "There are probably a lot of people that would come just to observe."

"No, but this guy was disgusted with the whole scene here. It was just very different than any other thoughts here," I tried to explain. "Some of the women were disgusted too. But, something was just different about this mind."

"You know it was a guy?" Daisy asked in surprise.

"Well, I think it was. I'm not certain," I said wondering what made me think it was a man. "I guess it had a masculine feel to it."

"Well, try to find it again," Jordan ordered. "He's here and we don't want to lose him if you've got a bead on him."

I closed my eyes and sifted through the minds trying to find the one that had caught my interest. We were a little ways away from the main action of this seedy nightmare, but there were plenty of people around. After flitting in and out of a few minds, I located it again. I opened my eyes in amazement and then closed them again.

"He's aware that we are here and he's also picking up on bits of our conversation," I thought to each of them. "I don't think we should talk anymore. I'll report my thoughts to Jordan right now and let you guys know what he wants you to do if he decides to make a move."

Everyone nodded their agreement. I drifted back into my quarry's mind. He was confused. He could smell a drainer and two healers. He didn't seem to notice my scent. Maybe because he was too intent on the drainers and healers together. The idea of this made him very wary. I guess the Alexander's little arrangement was as unusual as they claimed. This person had never heard of drainers and healers hanging around each other. He knew that sometimes the two mingled with humans undetected, but that was for work or other necessary reasons. He was definitely apprehensive about us. And, from the bits of our conversation he'd picked up, he suspected that we were talking about him.

I related my thoughts to Jordan and continued to follow his thoughts.

"Can you tell where he is?" Jordan asked in my head.

"No. He's focused inward and on his own senses, specifically hearing and smelling," I answered back into his head. "I can only see what he sees if he's thinking about it, and he's not."

Jordan nodded. "Keep trying. Let me know if you get anything else."

I was wide awake and hyper focused on my suspect when his mind seemed to jerk and a vision appeared in his mind. He was focused now on a man and a woman.

"Take it easy, sugar," the girl, who looked awfully young, was saying to the man in this guy's head. He was watching something unfold in front of him.

"I don't want to take it easy. I paid for it," the man said snatching the girl and slamming her into the wall of the building they were standing in front of. *"Now just shut up and give me what I paid for."*

I flinched and gasped at the amount of clarity I heard of the impact of the girl being slammed into the wall of the building from this drainers mind. She grunted in pain and began struggling in earnest as the man began groping and pulling at her. The impact of the violence unfolding in this drainers mind and his immediate response of rage, heightened my own response causing me to gasp for breath and grip the door handle. He wanted to go to the girl and help her, but his rage and anger was only rivaled by his fear of the drainers and healers he suspected where after him…, us. I was just getting ready to convey this to Jordan when I sensed the unanimous movement of all of the others in the car. My eyes flew open to see they'd all turned in the same direction, the movement seeming loud in the quiet car.

"What the hell?" Ethan said.

"The man. He's going to hurt her," I blurted out forgetting the caution of the agreement for silence in my need to help the woman somehow. "He sees it too, but is too afraid to help her."

"Oh, God," Daisy gasped. "We gotta help her. I can't sit here and watch this."

"Damn!" Jordan growled bursting out of the car with Ethan bursting out of the other side.

"You two stay here," Ethan ordered and then he and Jordan disappeared in a blur.

I couldn't see a damn thing. Daisy had immediately grabbed her phone and started texting. Then a moment later she placed a hand on my arm.

"Breath, Lela," she said in a soothing voice. "You always hold your breath when you get upset, you know that? Logan and the rest of them are on their way. Now, is our drainer still here?"

I'd forgotten about him. I took a deep breath and realized I was shaking. I focused my mind and searched for my suspect. He wasn't difficult to find. He was frozen with a combination of fear, shock, and confusion as he watched Jordan and Ethan descend on the man like a fury. What I couldn't see with my own eyes in the dark, I saw clearly in his mind. The controlled fury with which Jordan snatched the man, pulling him off of the girl and flinging him to the ground was astonishing. As strong as Jordan was with his super human strength, that move could have seriously hurt the man. The girl immediately tried to run once she was free of the man, but Ethan caught her gently. She began to fight like a wild thing when Ethan touched her, but he restrained her as gently as if she were a kitten as he murmured to her. The suspect almost came out of hiding to help the girl now, but he stopped himself. Then, I realized I could hear Ethan's words through this guy's mind.

"I'm not going to hurt you. You're safe now. No one is going to hurt you," he crooned to the terrified woman. She glanced past Ethan to see what was happening with her attacker. She stopped struggling when she saw that Jordan had the man face down on the ground with his hands neatly tied behind his back with plastic ties. Where the heck had he gotten those? Then suddenly the entire scene changed and the images flew by faster than I could see them. That was when I remembered I was watching all of this through someone else's mind. Someone who was blown away by what had just happened and didn't know what to make of it.

"Let's go," Daisy said grabbing my hand and practically dragging me from the car. "We need to help the guys with that girl at least. She's so terrified, the last thing she wants to see is another man. Our covers been blown anyway."

"Our guy took off just a few moments ago," I said. "He's freaked out by all of this. He was too scared to come to her rescue, but certainly wasn't expecting us too. He correctly surmised that we were after him, but doesn't know what to think now that

Jordan and Ethan rescued that girl. He's still afraid but really confused now."

"Well, we'll have to worry about him later," she said as we reached the guys. Daisy immediately headed for the woman. Seeing her with my own eyes was a little different than seeing her through our mysterious drainer's eyes. I guess I'd vaguely noticed that she had blood on her, but because it hadn't been so prominent in his mind, I hadn't noticed it before. She had a bloody nose and the side of her cheek where the man had slammed her face into the wall was scraped and swelling. Her hair was a mess and her clothes were torn. Ethan immediately released the woman and stepped away when Daisy took over restraining her. She tried to fight Daisy too, but she was obviously tired and appeared to be closer to tears now. Some of the terror had left her eyes, though she didn't take them away from her attacker for long.

Once Ethan had released the woman, he made his way to Jordan standing over the man. Jordan looked up finally and then looked over at Daisy and the woman. Then he did a double take. Wondering what had caught his eye, I noticed that the piece of cloth that had barely been passing for a shirt before her attacker had ripped it, was now exposing most of the girl's ample bosom. The next thing I knew, Jordan was pulling his own shirt over his head and handing it to Daisy. The girl stopped struggling against Daisy as if she finally realized she was safe and began to cry in earnest. Daisy slipped the shirt over her easily and held her while she cried.

Jordan then swung around to me and headed in my direction. I'd been standing there, rooted to the spot, as if watching a train wreck coming at me but unable to get out of the way.

"Are you alright?" Jordan asked approaching me cautiously. I shook myself and shut my senses down, realizing it was this young woman, this girls pain and terror, which was holding me captive.

"I'm fine," I said, the words coming out in a rush. He looked doubtful but Logan pulled in before he could say anything. Jordan grabbed my hand and gently pulled me over to Logan's car. He began reporting on everything that had happened, from me locating our suspect to the attack on the girl and his and Ethan's rescuing of her.

"Are you alright, Lela," Grace asked touching my arm quickly.

"I'm fine," I said toneless again as she frowned.

"You're a little shocky, but otherwise alright," she said pulling something out of the car and handing it to me. "Here. Put this on."

It was a light jacket. And, although it was still pretty warm outside, I realized I was standing there shivering and hugging myself.

"How do you want to do this, Jordan?" Logan asked.

Jordan turned an unsure look on me. "Lela, do you think you can sit in on interrogations?"

"Yes. Of course," I said feeling like I'd drank one too many cups of coffee.

"She's coming down from an adrenaline rush," Grace said to Jordan, Shane, and Logan who were all looking at me now with varying degrees of worry. "She'll be ok."

I took a deep breath. "I'm fine, really. I can sit in on the interviews."

"Ok, well, do you have an opinion on what we should do first?" Jordan asked pointedly.

"Uh, let me think," I said stalling. I knew what he was asking. Had I seen into either of their minds to see if they could tell us anything? I closed my eyes and cautiously probed the attacker's mind. He was furious and afraid that he'd been caught up in a raid. He was sweating bullets about what was going to happen to him, would he lose his job, and other such thoughts. I couldn't see where that would be helpful, so I got out of his caustic, ruthless mind. Then, I gingerly took a peak into the woman's mind.

"Is one of these guys the guardian? They have to be, but I thought he worked alone," she thought frantically, trying to make sense of what had just happened. *"The other girls said it was only one person that rescued them, not a team. Who are these people?"*

I opened my eyes to see everyone watching me except the man face down on the ground.

"She knows something. He's just upset." I conveyed my findings directly into Jordan's head. Then, I spoke aloud for the sake of the people around me who didn't know about my gift, which only consisted of the man on the ground and the terrified woman. "It's your call Jordan."

"Ok, I think we should drop this guy off with the local police," Jordan said. "We can take the girl with us. Grace could give her some medical attention."

"Alright then. Jordan you and the ladies please escort Miss…, ahem, her with you," he said gesturing to the woman. Then he turned to the man that had Beto's foot resting casually on his back. "And, we'll take him with us."

Beto jerked the man up onto his feet and led him away to Logan's car. Shane, Logan, and Ethan followed. They quickly loaded the man into the car and drove away. I turned now to see that Grace was kneeling in front of the woman.

"My name is Grace Alexander, and I'm a doctor. I'm here to help you," Grace was saying softly to the young woman. "Can you tell me your name?"

"A-A-Agnes," the girl stammered still looking wide eyed, but some of the wildness had left her eyes. I noticed that Daisy was still holding her, no doubt sending her some of her healing power. The girl's cheek looked less puffy. Grace pulled out one of those ice packs that you crush whatever is inside and they instantly get cold and handed it to her. But, I knew that Grace and Daisy's healing was what was going to make the biggest difference.

"Put this on your cheek, Agnes," Grace commanded smoothly. "It will help with the swelling. Now Agnes, I'd like to take you to my clinic and bandage your scrapes and bruises. Would that be ok?"

The girl nodded slowly.

"Good girl," Grace praised her. "We'll also get you some new clothes to wear and something to eat. Does that sound good?"

The girl simply nodded slowly again. And when Daisy rose pulling Agnes up with her, she stayed huddled into Daisy's side as if Daisy was her protection and she would not be parted from her. I sat up front with Jordan while Grace and Daisy settled themselves in the back of his SUV with Agnes.

Once we arrived at the ranch, Grace immediately started giving everyone their orders. "Daisy, please take her into the exam room. Jordan, can you please have someone make Agnes a plate of food. I'm pretty sure she's starving."

Daisy headed straight for the exam room with Agnes, while Jordan immediately headed for the kitchen. I was the only one left with nothing to do. Then Grace turned to me.

"Logan and the guys usually do the interrogations. They'll likely be back by the time I'm done with her. I'm just not sure she will respond to them," she said sounding concerned.

"I think she'll be fine with them. She thinks of them as her saviors. I don't know how she would respond to any of the other guys, but I'm pretty sure she'd respond to Ethan and Jordan."

"Good. That makes me feel better. I'm no good at interrogations," Grace said sounding relieved. "Let Logan and the rest know when they arrive. They should be here very soon. They were just dropping that scumbag off. And, this won't take very long. Just get comfortable while you can. You look exhausted."

I sat down right there in the plush receiving area near the front door. I vaguely wondered how any of them had the authority to just drop someone off at the police station, but decided I was too tired to care. Jordan came to join me after a few minutes. I told him about the conversation I'd just had with Grace. He agreed that he and Ethan should do the interrogation. Just as Grace had predicted, it wasn't long before the rest of the guys were coming through the door. Jordan filled them in and, in less than an hour after we'd arrived, they had Agnes in one of the offices with a plate of hot food in front of her.

Logan had asked if I wanted to sit in the room while they talked to the woman, but I couldn't. I needed some physical distance from her since I wouldn't be able to put mental distance between us. I was tired and my nerves where fried. I felt like I was barely hanging on. Tonight had been insane, and somehow I was just supposed to function like this was normal? I felt traumatized. So I sat in another room with Logan, Grace, and Daisy waiting for the interview to begin. The intercom on the phone in our room had been set so that we could hear the conversation inside the other room.

"I'll answer any questions you want me to," the girl said eagerly. I could feel her anxiety at not knowing what they wanted, and her need to please them. She really had a huge case of hero worship.

"That's good, Agnes. We appreciate that," Ethan was saying. "Go ahead and eat. We can talk to you while you are eating."

The girl began to devour the food with gusto. I gave myself a mental break from her mind as all she was thinking about now was food. Too wired to even think of food myself, Agnes' total focus on it was making me feel sick. I just couldn't even hear her think of eating right now. The other room was quiet for a few moments. I realized they were letting her eat. They must have picked up on her obviously acute hunger. After a few moments, her voice came over the speaker.

"I'm sorry. This is so good, and I am so hungry," she said sheepishly. I dove back into her head now that she was talking. "I don't have any money to pay you, but…"

She trailed off and my eyes widened as I realized where her thoughts were going. She had nothing else to offer them but herself! And, though she didn't like the idea of anyone touching her, she was willing to let them have their way with her. I switched to Ethan's head to warn him and felt his puzzlement. I could see her clearly now from his point of view and the girl was looking down at her lap.

"Ethan, she's going to-" was as far as I got before the girl had grabbed the hem of Jordan's shirt that he'd let her borrow when her shirt was torn. She was pulling it up. Ethan and Jordan both shot out of their chairs.

"No, Agnes. Um, that's not necessary," came Jordan's startled voice as Ethan firmly grabbled Agnes hands and pulled the shirt back down. I switched to Jordan's head to find him cringing internally. I wondered what he looked like on the outside. Probably calm and collected as usual. From Jordan's view however, I could see that Agnes had a completely baffled and unsure look on her face. The whole thing would have been funny if it wasn't so tragic. I switched back to Agnes' head.

"What just happened?" Beto asked. I didn't open my eyes and I didn't answer. I'd let the guys explain that one when they came out.

"I don't understand," Agnes was saying. "What do you 'all want from me?"

"We only want information. That's all," Jordan said hastily. "We just want to ask you a few questions."

"Ok," Agnes replied still unsure.

"Agnes, did you know the man that attacked you?" Ethan asked.

"No. I didn't know him. He was just a customer."

The room was quiet for a moment and Agnes' uneasiness was growing. I switched to Jordan's mind. I could feel him trying to figure out a way to ask her about "the savior" thought I'd told him I picked up from her. He was trying to bring it up without spooking her.

"Agnes, have you been having problems with customers like the man who attacked you lately?" Jordan asked.

"We always have problems with customers like him. Some of the girls tell horrible stories. Some of them don't make it."

"What do you girls do to try and protect yourselves?" Ethan asked.

"Well, some girls try to carry something they can use as a weapon," she said thinking. "But, lately, a few of the girls have been saved by some kind of superhero."

"A superhero?" Jordan asked.

"Yes. If one of the girls is in trouble, he seems to just come out of nowhere and rescue them." She was clearly wondering if one of them was the person she was referring to, but was too afraid to ask.

"Have you seen this superhero?" Jordan asked.

"No. I mean, not until tonight," she hinted, hoping one of them would confess to being him.

There was the sound of paper rustling through the speaker in the room. Through Agnes' thoughts, I could see Jordan pulling pictures from a manila envelope. I tensed, but realized they weren't pictures of the dead men from the case files. Somehow, the Alexanders had obtained what looked like driver's license photos. He placed the photos in front of Agnes.

"Have you ever seen any of these men before?" Jordan continued the questioning.

"No," Agnes said becoming excited. She somehow thought that the fact that they had pictures of these men was proof that she was meeting the superhero the other girls had been telling her about. "Are these the men that you, I mean, the superhero guy rescued the other girls from?"

"We aren't the superhero who saved those girls," Ethan explained. "But, we think that these are the men that they were saved from."

"Oh," Agnes said sounding a little disappointed. "Well, I never saw the men or the superhero. I only heard about it."

"So, you know the girls that were saved by the superhero?" Ethan asked.

"Yes. That's all they talk about."

"Do you think that you could get them to talk to us about these men?" Ethan asked.

"Sure, if it would mean that they'd never be able to hurt anyone again, if they know those men would be locked up. I think they wouldn't mind talking at all, especially after I tell them how you saved me, fed me, bandaged my wounds, and wouldn't let me pay you."

Jordan choked and then cleared his throat. "We can personally guarantee that they won't bother you ladies anymore. We just need your friends to identify them. That would help us out a great deal."

I was almost impressed at the way Jordan had neatly stated the truth, yet made it sound like something else entirely without being a lie. Clearly he didn't want to tell Agnes that the men were dead, since she didn't seem to already know. I had to agree that this was probably a good thing. I wasn't sure how she'd react to knowing her superhero savior was also a killer. She might be fine with it. Then again, it might just freak her out. Better not to chance it.

"What exactly did your friends say happened?" Ethan took up the questioning.

Agnes explained that in each case, one of the girls had been being knocked around or handled roughly by a customer when they were rescued. She went on to explain that none of the girls had stuck around to see what happened. As soon as they were free, they ran for their lives.

With that, the interview came to a close. Grace had arranged for someone to come pick Agnes up and take her to a safe place for the night. Apparently Agnes would have the option to join some program that helped get women off the streets and gainfully employed in a safer line of work. I just hoped Agnes chose that option.

Before Jordan had taken me home, we'd had a brief meeting where I'd given them all of the information I had. Agnes had told them the complete truth. She hadn't held anything back in answering their questions. If she knew anything else she hadn't told them, they simply hadn't asked the right question to retrieve the information.

I explained to them that our suspect had found us right away. He had not only been confused that drainers and healers seemed to be working together, but he'd been afraid and baffled by everything that unfolded before he bolted. Logan decided we would have to do it again, but do a better job of staying off of our suspect's radar. It was determined that it had been a bad idea to sit with the windows rolled down. If Jordan, Ethan and Daisy could smell him, then he could also smell all of them.

"Why didn't he smell you?" Logan asked me.

"I'm not sure he didn't. I just think he didn't think about it because I would just be another human in the area. He clearly didn't associate my smell with theirs, at least not consciously."

He nodded, "Good job tonight. We just might be getting somewhere now."

Logan dismissed everyone saying that we would meet again tomorrow evening and plan how to approach the next stakeout. I was bone tired and exhausted. Jordan ushered me into his car and took me home. It was a quiet ride home. I headed straight for the shower when I got home.

Not trusting Jordan to behave and too tired to fight with him, I tried to send him home.

"I'm not leaving you alone, Lela," he said with grim determination. "Now go take your shower and get in the bed. Trust me, I know you aren't up for anything but sleep tonight."

When I came out of the bathroom, Jordan had taken up his usual position on the other side of my bed. It was now well into the morning hours, and I felt too keyed up to sleep. After the night I'd had, I couldn't close my eyes without being thrown into a nightmare recap of the last few hours.

Thankfully Jordan was true to his word. He simply pulled me into his arms in a comforting hold. I was out as soon as I hit the pillow.

Chapter 16

The next morning I didn't go into my office until eleven. These long nights and getting up in the morning for work was killing me.

"Take some time off," Jordan suggested as he coaxed me out of bed with coffee and a pastry.

"I don't have unlimited time off, Jordan," I grumbled. "I can't just keep taking time off. Between my vacation, the previous case, and this one, I'm probably getting a little low."

"For the last case you worked, Logan made arrangements for you to be at the Ranch with us. That shouldn't have used any of your vacation."

"Well, I can't keep doing that either."

"Why not? We pay your job and you for your services," Jordan said clearly not understanding.

"Because it really isn't company business, Jordan," I explained. "You know what? I'm too tired to even think about this right now. I have to go to work."

I gave Jordan a quick kiss goodbye and headed out the door.

After another busy day at work, it was now five o'clock, and I was headed home. Knowing I'd be picked up in a few short hours for our nightly stake out, I went right to bed to get a few hours of sleep. This time Jordan woke me up after only an hour to tell me that he was on his way. I hadn't even bothered to change my work clothes before falling across my bed. So, I went back to sleep until Jordan and the gang arrived to pick me up at seven thirty. Logan needed everyone to come earlier than our previous nights to explain a new development and decide how to proceed tonight.

I was finally dragged from my bed and herded to the car after I failed to answer the door. Those darn Alexanders could get into Fort Knox. I hadn't actually been ignoring the doorbell or the pounding on the door. I just hadn't heard it.

When we arrived at the ranch, everyone was assembled in the conference room. Once Jordan and I took our seats, Logan started talking.

"We've decided to keep the same teams we had yesterday but switch locations," Logan was saying.

"Why?" Shane asked. "We could have had our guy last night if we hadn't gotten distracted saving Agnes. Tonight we can just be prepared to save someone and still catch our guy."

"Another woman was found dead this morning. This girl was actually a college student," Logan explained grimly. "We think he may have smelled us like Lela explained that our other suspect smelled you guys. He must have gotten spooked and decided to take his hunting elsewhere."

Logan picked up the television remote and pointed it towards the flat screen on the wall at the front of the conference room. He then clicked a few buttons showing a list of recordings and chose one. It was a news report on a girl found dead near her off campus apartment. Alissa James had been found sitting on a park bench as if she were asleep. They showed a picture of a pretty brown haired woman with a broad smile. The authorities had no idea why she died. Then the sound and images of her distraught parents came on the screen, and my stomach knotted and twisted. Her parents were stoically trying to keep it together, but their tear stained faces and puffy, red eyes expressed their grief all too well. Thankfully Logan clicked off the television and the screen went blank.

"We know that the suspect who has been killing the men appears to be only attacking the ones who are being too aggressive, or are harming the girls. Grace, Shane, Beto and I know his scent from the dead bodies he's left us, but he doesn't know ours. He knows yours," Logan stated pointing at Jordan, Daisy and Ethan. "We might have the element of surprise with him. Regardless, I would rather have you there to see if we can get any information on the suspect killing the women, Lela. I think we can save the scumbags roughing up the women and also keep the women safe. But, we know nothing about our other suspect, so there's no one to keep the women safe from him."

This made sense to me. Waves of anguish and grief tried to crash into me. That girl was dead because of me. If I had been there last night, she might still be alive.

"I see what you mean," Shane agreed. "And our woman killer won't know our scents either, but we know his. So, if we pick up on his scent then we may be able to catch him."

"Exactly," Logan said. "So, let's head out. We can be in the city in the next thirty minutes."

Tonight wasn't quite as warm as the night before, but it was still too warm to be holed up in the car with the windows up. Jordan, Ethan, and Daisy took turns opening their windows only a crack and scenting the air. It was agreed that they should not keep the windows open to allow their scents to drift out freely. In the meantime, I randomly searched the minds of the people in the area. After an hour, I picked up on a thought. Someone was there, scenting the air also, and I could almost smell what they smelled. He was searching for someone. His mind was very cautious.

"I think he's here," I whispered into the silence of the car.

"Where?" Daisy asked.

"I'm not sure. I'm not familiar with the area so I don't know what I am looking at, or rather, what he is looking at," I answered. "But, he's looking for someone, and he's afraid to come out."

They all rolled down their windows slightly to try and catch the scent.

"*I think I smell him,*" Ethan thought to me just as the suspect got his own whiff of one of them and bolted.

"He bolted," I whispered into the car. Ethan, Daisy, and Jordan all turned to me as they rolled their windows up.

"Where is he going?" Daisy asked.

"I have no idea," I said. "He took off after he seemed to pick up your scent, Jordan. His thought wasn't exactly clear, but he seemed to recognize there was a drainer here somewhere. When he started running I lost him. I'm sorry, his mind got into a crazy panic. With all the movement, everything was jumbled and it hurt. I flinched and lost him."

"Should we try to track him?" Daisy asked.

"I'm tempted to," Jordan stated thoughtfully. "But, I don't think we should try. There's a bit of a breeze tonight, which would make tracking a little hard. We'd have to split up and Ethan and I are the only ones who can really track well. I think it would be a better idea to see if he returns to where the girl was found this morning. He might go back there to look for a new victim. We might keep someone safe tonight."

So we spent the next few hours patrolling the area around the college until Logan called in to have us call it a night. Nothing was happening and he had called in secondary teams to relieve us. This way, both areas would be being patrolled. Logan asked us to drive by their stake out site and see if I could pick up on anything before we all headed back to the ranch.

"Be careful to keep your windows up and your scent inside the car," Logan's voice ordered through the speakers of the car via Bluetooth as we drove in his direction. Sure enough, I picked up on the mind of the man killer who'd been there last night. He was there and he didn't seem to know that Logan and his team were there. After this was confirmed, Logan ordered everyone back to the ranch for a briefing. He left instructions for his replacement team to capture our suspect if he came out of hiding to protect any of the women, but the night had been a slow one. There weren't any customers out tonight. Or at least there weren't any that were attacking anyone.

Chapter 17

"We were careful not to let our man killing suspect detect us. We kept the windows rolled up but had the fan on in the car blowing in the outside air," Logan was saying. "We picked up his scent, but we didn't know where he was. And, all of the customers were on their best behavior so far tonight, so he had no need to come out and rescue anyone. So, I'd like to come up with a plan of attack for our two issues with this suspect. We need to go undetected by him, and we need something to happen to force him to come out. If we come out after him, he'll bolt before we ever figure out where he is."

"Daisy could pose undercover as one of the girls," Ethan suggested.

"Thanks, Ethan," Daisy retorted with false cheer.

"You're welcome," he smiled brightly before turning back to the room. "And I can attack her."

"That probably wouldn't work," Grace said doubtfully. "He'll know you both are healers. We aren't dealing with a normal here. If we were, he'd be much easier to catch."

"True," Ethan frowned.

"We could probably use a couple of our human staff," Daisy suggested.

"That might be too dangerous," Grace frowned.

"Agreed," Logan said. "We'd have to be very careful in order to keep our guys safe. Our suspect is a drainer. A normal man attacker wouldn't stand a chance against him. We'd have to be able to get to him before our suspect did, otherwise we could end up with another dead body. And, we'd need our woman to be able to have some fighting skill, or be willing to fight back to make it look real."

"And a normal woman with one of our drainer staff wouldn't work either. The take down wouldn't be as easy with a drainer on drainer fight," Beto added. "The woman would know that something wasn't quite normal. We already have a group of prostitutes talking about a superhero. We definitely don't need to add to the rumors."

"I could do it," I blurted out realizing what they needed. They needed a normal human female so that our suspect would know she needed help. But, they needed one who already knew about their little secret. I was the obvious choice.

"No you can't," Jordan barked turning an incredulous gaze on me. "It's way too dangerous for you."

"Not if it's one of our guys," Ethan said. "Lela can hold her own against another human and make it look real. And the only person who will really be in danger is our guy. This guy protects the women and kills the men, remember?"

"We can't use a normal male for the same reason we can't use a normal female," Jordan argued. "And we can't use a drainer attacker because our suspect would pick up on the scent and not come to help her. So, we need another plan."

"Not if Shane was the attacker," Daisy said thoughtfully. Everyone turned to Daisy.

"Why wouldn't he smell Shane?" Beto asked. "I smell him."

"That's because you know him and know exactly what he is," Daisy replied. "But, how long did it take you to figure out he was a healer when you first met him?"

"Yea, I see what you're saying," Beto replied. "His scent is so mild. Even if you do notice it you aren't sure if he is a healer, or if he's just spent some time around one and the scent is on him."

"Exactly," Daisy said. "His doesn't register more than someone who has had casual contact with a healer if you pick it up at all. His normal human scent masks it well."

"We could probably mask his scent even more," Grace chimed in. "Shane, if you could wear some freshly worn clothes of some of your normal family, or anyone for that matter, you would simply smell more like a normal that has come in contact with a healer. That's a fairly normal occurrence."

"That's all well and good, but Lela isn't doing this," Jordan stated firmly. "It's too dangerous."

"Jordan!" I frowned. "First of all, it is more dangerous for my attacker than me. Remember this guy is killing the attackers not the women. Second, you need a normal woman to play the part that already knows about your secret. I won't be shocked into oblivion by seeing the take down. Lastly, Shane and I can choreograph a fight or struggle better since we spar all of the time."

"No, Lela. You aren't doing this," Jordan said heatedly.

"Excuse me?" I shot back turning completely to face him. "You don't get to decide what I can and cannot do."

"You are not going to be put out there to wait for some jon to come knock you around and some drainer to come save you," Jordan growled right back.

"That's not what we're suggesting," Grace said.

"Like hell it's not," Jordan snapped.

"Let's just all take a deep breath," Logan said before Jordan could respond and further escalate our argument. No one spoke for a long moment.

"The plan could work," Ethan said into the void, breaking the silence.

"There are people dying out there," I said trying to speak in a reasonable voice to Jordan. "I will be perfectly safe. You can't let your overprotectiveness cloud your judgment here, Jordan. Think about it."

"And, it's not like she and Shane will be alone," Logan assured Jordan. "We will have our team there ready for the take down. The moment he comes out, we will have him. But, this also ensures the safety of all of our people. Using a normal man is too risky."

"So, you're saying you'd volunteer to put Grace in harm's way?" Jordan turned his anger onto his brother.

"No, Jordan," Logan said patiently. "But, I'd be smart enough to realize it's her decision. And, I'd support her as long as I knew that she would be safe. This particular situation doesn't apply anyway. Grace could protect herself. Regardless, we are not putting Lela in harm's way. Calm down Jordan."

"I'll do it," I said turning back to Logan. It was quiet as everyone looked to see Jordan's reaction. He just sat there fuming for a few more moments.

"If she's going out there, I am going to be a part of the team for the take down," Jordan finally gritted out.

"I'm not sure it's a good idea for you to go, Jordan," Grace said cautiously.

"I'm going, Grace," Jordan said giving her a steely look. "And, she can't be out of my line of sight."

"I'm fine with that as long as you are able to keep your head, Jordan," Logan said before Grace could express any more doubt. "Lela and Shane are going to have to make this as convincing as possible."

"I can handle it," Jordan bit out.

"Ok, then," Logan agreed.

So it was settled. We talked more about logistics and who would be coming along. We decided that I'd better drive myself, and probably not in my own car since Jordan, Daisy, and Ethan's smells were in my car. I decided to use Blake's car. No one but us normals had ever been in Blake's car. It was also decided that Shane should drive himself as well. He said he could use one of his relative's car. His mother was the only healer, so he could use some of the clothes and the car of a cousin and smell very regular. With those details taken care of, Shane and I agreed to focus on some of the defensive sparring techniques we used the most. It was late, but we agreed it wouldn't be wise to get together tomorrow. We didn't want to risk our scents already being mingled on us when we arrived at the take down site. After some strategic planning with Shane, I was sent home to get some rest.

Knowing that I needed to get more sleep, I planned to only work a half day the next day. Jordan and I had gone to bed a little earlier tonight, at one in the morning, but I couldn't sleep. I was totally out of gas, but my mind would not quiet and still enough for me to go to sleep.

"Babe, why aren't you sleep?" Jordan asked. We were spooning as usual and his breath tickled my ear as he spoke.

"I don't know. I guess my mind is still racing."

He lifted up on his elbow and rolled me to my back so he could see my face. "What are you thinking about? Are you worried about tomorrow? You don't have to do it, Lela. I'd really prefer you didn't."

I reached up and touched my finger to his mouth to quiet him. "I'm not worried about tomorrow, Jordan. You are the one worrying over that."

"Then, what's bothering you?"

"That girl. She died because of me, Jordan," I said feeling a lump form in my throat.

"What girl?" he frowned.

"The student. If I had been there, she would still be alive," I explained and felt tears welling in my eyes. I knew I was being irrational. I was so tired, I was practically delirious. But, even though my rational side explained this to me, my emotional side was not getting the memo.

"Lela, honey, you can't blame yourself for that," Jordan said trying to comfort me. "If you had been there, then maybe Agnes would be dead now."

"No, because Logan's team would have rescued her," I disagreed.

"You don't know that. Don't do this to yourself," he said pulling me to him. "You can't be everywhere at one time."

"They found her on a park bench, Jordan," I sniffled. "And her parents will never know she was murdered. We didn't save her."

"I know," he said wiping the tears from my face with his thumb. "It really is awful. And, that's why we are going to get this guy."

"I know it's irrational and doesn't make sense," I sniffled, my tears flowing now. "This is what happens when I don't get enough sleep. I become an emotional basket case."

"Come here," he said and wrapped his arms around me. Then he captured my lips in a soft, sweet kiss. He coaxed and teased my mouth causing me to focus all of my attention on the kiss.

I knew what Jordan was doing, yet I couldn't stop myself from accepting the comfort he was offering. I knew I was allowing myself to lean on Jordan way too much lately for emotional comfort and support. What had begun as something very physical between us was turning into something much more. Something I was loathe to define.

Jordan was gentle with me tonight. He always seemed to know exactly what I needed. He wiped my tears away with his thumbs and then placed gentle kisses on my eyes. Pulling me to my side and against him we faced each other. He rubbed gently along my spine in a soothing motion as he coaxed my mouth open again for his kiss. He didn't rush, but he didn't tease.

When I sighed and relaxed into him he rolled us over so that I as on my back and he was nestled between my legs. His hands roamed lazily over me, massaging in gentle circles as they went over my breasts, down my side and to my hip where he made lazy circles before squeezing gently.

It was me who began moving against him, but he didn't make me wait. He stripped my pajama bottoms off and resettled himself beside me. He slid those magical finger up the inner part of my thigh until he reached his destination. Finding me more than ready for him, he positioned himself above me and eased himself slowly and deeply inside me. He set a slow pace that had me coming apart much faster than his more frantic lovemaking sessions. Jordan knew how to hold me right on the edge and have me begging to be released. He didn't do that tonight though. Every stroke, every caress, and every kiss was gentle, soothing and passionate.

He continued to move, not altering his pace as I arched against him crying out from my own climax. And then he had me building, yearning, and gasping all over again. By the time Jordan finally relaxed his own self-restraint and sent us both over the edge for the final time I was spent. My mind was clear and my body was totally relaxed.

"Sleep," he whispered into my hair as he pulled me close. And that's exactly what I did.

Chapter 18

When I woke the next morning, I heard Jordan grinding coffee beans in the kitchen. I felt a pang of unwelcome disappointment that he wasn't still beside me. It was nine o'clock. No doubt Jordan had waited as long as he could for me to wake up. I knew he would have a lot to do today also.

"Hope you slept well," he said as he walked in my room with two cups of coffee in his hand a few moments later. He handed one to me. "Missing you already. See you this evening."

"Ok," I said smiling up at him as I took the mug he offered. He bent to give me a goodbye kiss and then was gone.

When I finally did see Jordan later in the day, he was a bit out of sorts. He'd met me at my house after work and was filling me in on the day's happenings. They'd located the other women Agnes had told them about and brought them in for questioning. The women were able to identify the men as their attackers. Unfortunately, that information didn't shed any new light on our suspect. The women knew nothing about him. They couldn't even give a description.

"Well, they may have had some information I could have gotten if you guys would have called me. They might have had some flickering images or thoughts I could have picked up," I complained.

"Maybe," he agreed. "But, you needed your rest. And, whatever little bit you would have been able to get from their minds wouldn't have been as useful as what we could get from you being there tonight."

"So you admit that, do you?" I grinned. "You admit that our plan could work?"

"I never doubted it could work," he grimaced. "I simply stated that I don't like this, Lela."

"You don't trust Shane to keep me safe?" I ask incredulously.

"Oh, I do. That's about the only thing I do trust him to do," Jordan said sounding disgruntled.

"What are you saying?"

"You know he has a thing for you, Lela," Jordan said dead pan. "So, now he gets to play the role of a jon picking you up as a hooker? Come on! Sounds like some twisted fantasy."

I stared at him with my mouth open for a few moments before my brain and mouth started working again. Was he serious?

"Shane is not like that. He hasn't done anything but completely back off once he got the slightest hint of us being involved. I'm sure he wouldn't do anything but his job," I defended.

"I'm sure he'll do his job too, especially since it means getting his hands on you," Jordan grumbled. "I don't want him touching you."

"Oh, Jordan, please," I said in disbelief. "Are you saying you don't trust Shane? I mean, what could he do anyway with you guys all looking on?"

"No. I don't trust him. Shane's a good guy. I know that," he said putting a hand up to stop my protest. "But, he *is* a guy. A guy that is very attracted to you. I don't trust him not to give in to the temptation of you."

"But, what about me?" I asked feeling a little insulted. "Are you saying you don't trust me either?"

"No. I do trust you," he said quickly, but I wasn't sure I completely believed him. I took a deep breath and searched for patience.

"Jordan, you are going to be right there," I said calmly. "If you stop and think about the whole plan, and the team executing it, I think you'll see that this is probably our best option. It could very well work."

He looked up to the ceiling as if he were now the one seeking patience. After expelling a long breath, he looked down at me and into my eyes.

"I know you are right. But, it still bothers me," he confessed. "Still, I'm sure everything will go fine."

"Logan called me today and said Shane wouldn't agree to do it unless you were ok with it," I informed Jordan.

"Logan has a big mouth," he replied.

"So, did you give Shane the ok?" I asked.

"I told Logan to tell Shane that I was fine with it. Just because I don't like it personally doesn't mean I can't see the merits of the plan," he replied grumpily. "At least you know how I feel about it."

"Duly noted."

Chapter 19

When Jordan left, I made sure to take another shower and put the clothes I'd be wearing tonight back on. I'd worn them all day under my work clothes. I had showered this morning when I'd awakened. I made sure to double wash so I wouldn't have any of Jordan's lingering smell on me after. After the last fiasco when I'd apparently been a walking advertisement of my nightly activities, I wasn't taking any chances. I had to make every effort to ensure that I'd have no lingering scent from any of the Alexanders. I'd worked all day in these clothes and made sure to have contact with animals and people.

When I'd arrived home from work, I'd changed into more comfortable clothes while Jordan was there. But, once Jordan left, I showered, yet again, and put my outfit back on. It was a lot of effort, but I knew first hand just how sensitive their noses could be.

I drove Blake's car. He'd left it at home and had the airport shuttle come and pick him up. My only issue was that I hated driving in the city. The lanes seemed too narrow, there were too many cars, and I didn't really know where I was going. Unless someone else was driving, this was the only destination in which I'd much rather brave public transportation in the bay area than drive. Oh, well. It couldn't be helped. After printing out my directions, I was on my way.

Jordan insisted on being no more than a mile away with a clear view of where I was to be. I had no idea where he actually was, but I had no doubt he knew where I was. I wondered what he would say when he saw the outfit I was wearing.

Apparently, Daisy had picked it out and had it delivered to me. I'd worn my little skimpy, barely there outfit all day at work under my regular work attire. It had been a warm day, which made for me being hot and uncomfortable in two layers of clothing. However, not wanting anyone to see me walking out of work looking like a street walker, I waited until I reached my house to remove my blouse and business skirt. I'd exchanged my serviceable work shoes for a pair of lethally high heels before heading out on my second shift of the night.

I arrived without incident at the agreed upon destination. Though I could walk in heels, I wasn't a heels kind of girl most of the time. If sore feet was required to be cute, then I just didn't need to be that cute. So, this had better happen quickly, or I'd be walking around barefoot. I pulled my hair from its ponytail and put on some overdone make up. I looked in the mirror, decided I looked garish enough, and sent the required text message to the group that I was going in.

I opened my senses right away as I walked down the street to my destination. I wasn't in the heart of the activity, but I was making my way to the outskirts of it. As I made my way closer to the busier areas, I got a few dirty looks from the regulars. So far, I hadn't picked up on our suspect. I strutted slowly a little farther in and decided to turn around and make my way back. Even knowing that I had a whole team watching me, I still felt creeped out. There was a lot of strange stuff going on that I didn't want a closer look at.

I was taking my time flitting through minds. I was on the lookout for two things and two things only, a danger to myself or my target. There were way too many sick and twisted things going through these minds around here. Some of them were likely stone crazy.

My feet were already starting to ache. I was just preparing to cross the street and walk along the other side when I picked up our suspects mind. He was just observing the scene before him, and he wasn't watching me. I reached into my phone to send my one word message to everyone. We'd agreed that I would send a text that simply stated "here" when, and if, I detected our suspect. That would let them know that I'd picked up on our suspects mind and also give Shane his cue to enter.

I walked over to one of the buildings near an alley. I tried to covertly inspect the wall of the building for filth before I leaned against it, trying to appear casually bored. There weren't a lot of people out, so I didn't want to walk all the way down to where Shane would take me by myself. Not that anyone around here would probably lift a finger to help if someone decided to attack me in plain sight on the street. I tried to stifle a shudder at the thought and picked at my nails. I was just about to dig in my little purse for a piece of gum for effect, when Shane pulled up in an old, but serviceable, Honda Accord. He rolled his window down and looked at me blankly. We hadn't thought about a script. The thought hadn't even occurred to me until now with Shane looking tongue tied. But, clearly our suspect would be able to hear our conversation. I sighed realizing we would have to wing it.

"You lost or looking for someone?" I asked with one brow raised, trying to sound jaded and bored. Shane said nothing. He just sat there gawking.

"You have to say something, Shane," I said into his head and he jerked like someone had shocked him. I realized then that I'd never spoken into his head before.

"Uh," was all that came out.

"Look sugar, if you want to just look that's fine, but it will still cost you," I said trying to prompt his brain. Was I going to have to do all of the work?

"Oh, I want a lot more than that," Shane finally said sounding a bit stiff. I eyed his car doubtfully for a minute before shifting my eyes back to him.

"I don't think you can afford much more than a look," I said trying to sound as doubtful as I hoped I was looking.

"How much?" Shane asked.

How the hell should I know? How did one even figure out what the going rate for sexual favors was? On second thought, that was another thing I didn't think I wanted to know.

"More than what you got," I said, stalling. This was awful.

Shane pulled out a hundred dollar bill and waved it through the window. "Get in," he ordered.

"Na, uh," I said shaking my head. "You want some of this, you get out. I'm not gettin' in your car."

I searched around to find our suspect and found that he was indeed watching us, though with no real interest. Ok, time to turn up the heat then.

"He's watching us, Shane," I thought in his head. *"Time to step it up here before we lose him."*

147

"Ok. We'll do it your way," Shane said stepping out of the car. He placed the hundred dollar bill in the cleavage of my shirt. "I've had a real rough week, so I hope you like it rough."

If it weren't for the mean look on his face, I would probably have laughed at his words. Our dialogue needed some major help. Shane grabbed my arm roughly and began dragging me down the street.

"No!" I said stumbling forward into him and then twisting my hand free of his grasp. "I don't do rough. Take your money!"

I snatched the money from my shirt and threw it down at his feet. We definitely had our suspect's full attention now. I spun on my heels and began to walk away, only to have Shane snatch me by the arm spinning me back around to face him. I lost my balance in the heels and cried out. Shane immediately caught me. I hoped our suspect didn't see the look of concern on his face.

"Let go of me," I yelled at him. He hesitated as if trying to determine if we were still acting or not, and I snatched my arm from him yet again.

"Hey," he said a little too gently and a little to quietly to sound mean. He touched my arm lightly. I swung around and punched him in the arm.

"I said I don't do rough!" I snarled. "Take your money and move on."

Shane looked shocked as I spun around and walked away. I sighed inwardly. This was clearly not an easy thing for Shane.

His feelings of caution and concern were making it hard for me to keep my attention on our suspect.

"Come on, Shane. I'm getting away," I coaxed in his mind. *"If you think directly at me, I'll pick up your thoughts. If you want to know if I'm ok, just ask. Now can you get a little mean?"*

The next thing I knew, I was grabbed and hauled down the street.

"As long as you promise to tell me if I'm hurting you or something is wrong," came his reply right into my head.

I paused in all of my verbal protesting, finding that I couldn't actually speak my protests and send him a completely different thought at the same time. *"I promise."* I thought to him as he dragged me unceremoniously down the street.

"Get your hands off of me!" I yelled as I twisted, kicked, and fought to free myself. Our suspect was not only paying attention, but I could feel his concern rising. Though, something was holding him back. I'd have to say he was a good judge of character. He seemed to doubt that Shane would really hurt me.

We struggled as Shane dragged me down the street and he finally got me into a come along hold and continued dragging me further down the street. I fought as best I could without doing anything to show that I could actually break his hold. When we arrived at the designated spot, Shane very carefully shoved me towards the wall of the building in an alley. I exaggerated my steps and staggered into the side wall of the building where the rest of this ordeal was to take place away from too many eyes. It was dark in the alley and I couldn't see a thing. I knew, however, that Shane could see just fine.

"It's clear," he said mentally as if reading my mind. I relaxed knowing there wasn't some addict or other crazy person in the alley with us. And, I knew that Logan and the rest of them were also nearby. I focused in on our suspect and felt his fear and anxiety for me growing. Still, mingled in with his concern for me was some nagging doubt telling him that something wasn't right. I could only imagine it was Shane's reluctant performance. Shane kept lunging for me, but I was easily able to fend him off. We were doing more fighting than anything else. Shane was clearly a reluctant attacker.

"Shane, we are going to lose him. Stop being so reluctant," I urged. *"You're going to have to pin me or something. Come at me harder."*

"What the hell else do you want me to do? I'm not going to beat you up!" he thought back. I could hear his agitation and frustration growing.

"You aren't here to beat me up. You are here for sex, remember?" I thought back. *"And, you aren't taking no for an answer. Now, it's show time. You gotta go for it."*

"How did I get myself into this," he thought to himself with mental anguish. Then I felt him steeling himself to do what needed to be done. Realizing I was now focusing on Shane instead of our suspect, I cast my senses around again until I found my

150

target. He was still there but almost ready to decide that Shane wouldn't hurt me. Then, Shane suddenly grabbed me and slammed me into the wall of the building, getting both my attention and our suspects. I noticed he was careful to cradle my head so that his hand took the blow against the building and not my head.

"What are you doing?" I asked in a panic. He'd caught me off guard, so I didn't have to fake it to make my panic sound real. "Let me go."

"Didn't I tell you? I like it rough," Shane growled at me and grabbed my flimsy shirt. The fabric ripped in his hands revealing the tank top I had under it. I had worn a tank top under it for just this purpose, but I have to admit, it still startled me. I tried to scream and he clamped a hand over my mouth. I opened my eyes wide and tried to imagine real terror to make it as real as possible. It must have worked, because I thought I caught a flicker of unease in Shane's eyes. His eyes widened and he hesitated, releasing my mouth before pinning my hands above my head, lifting me against the wall and holding me there with his body and burying his face in my neck. I began to struggle for all I was worth.

"*Are you ok? You know I'm not really going to hurt you, right?*" Came Shane's worried voice in my head as he kept his head buried in my neck and my body pinned against the wall.

I froze at his words, now taken out of my terrified character.

"I'm totally fine, Shane. I'll let you know if I'm not ok," I responded into his mind and began struggling against him in earnest again.

"Let me go!" I yelled and wriggled wildly against him, trying to free my hands and buck him away from me. He pressed deeper into me and re-clamped a hand over my mouth and squeezed my jaw more gently than was necessary. Still, I had to give him credit for the menacing look on his face as he raised his head to glare at me. It helped keep me in character.

"Look, I'm paying you and you agreed. Now just shut up and it will be over soon," he hissed at me. He must have seen the amusement in my eyes because he narrowed his own at me. I sure hoped the drainer was buying this, because Shane was clearly having a hard time roughing me up. I was able to buck him off and hit him square in the chest. I didn't want to appear to have any self-defense training, so it wasn't a very hard hit. We did a bit of sparing and grappling.

"Shit! What the hell do I have to do to you to get this guy to make a move?" Shane was practically yelling his frustration in my head.

"He's watching, Shane. And, he's agitated but unsure." I thought back. *"Look, I know you aren't going to hurt me. You come at*

me harder than this in practice. Just go for it. Stop holding back. Push him over the edge already. I promise to tell you if it's too much."

"*You want me to fight you?*"

"*No. I need to look weak and more defenseless. You want sex, right? You're going to have to come and get it.*"

"*What?*" he literally yelled in my head. I winced.

"*Not for real, dumbass!*" I thought back and kicked him hard in the stomach. "*You're supposed to be paying for it remember? Well, act like you intend to get what you paid for.*"

He staggered back and looked at me stunned for a moment. I stared back at him with what I hoped was a terrified expression and not a glare.

"*Come on, Shane! Let's do this,*" I roared at him in his head. He winced, and then narrowed his eyes.

I turned and tried to run. Shane caught me up and we both went sprawling. Then, he jumped up and grabbed me by my hair. This was nothing we hadn't practiced in training. Shane always tried to cover any scenario. I sprang to my feet as he pulled, so that he wouldn't actually be pulling me up by my hair, and he swung me around to throw me back into the wall. Again, I exaggerated the movement to make it look worse than it was. He grabbed me by the throat and squeezed gently. I pretended not to be able to breath and scratched at his hand. He again lifted me against the wall with his other hand and pressed into me. We were now groin to groin. I tried to struggle and look terrified. It was when he buried his head in my neck and began to move against me that all hell broke loose.

The first thing I noticed was the feeling of something rapidly growing rigid and pressing into me right as Shane groaned, cursed, and gentled his hold on me. Then, my head exploded with Grace, Logan, Ethan, and Daisy all screaming in my head at once. It was literally like taking a blow to the head, and I went weak in Shane's hold.

"Jordan's losing it," Daisy was thinking.

"Holly shit, Lela. I don't think we can hold Jordan much longer," came Ethan's thoughts.

"If you are ok, for heaven's sake, please tell Jordan before he takes the car apart," Logan was thinking.

"I'm fine, Jordan. Calm down," I said calmly, trying to breathe through the pain in my head from them all bombarding me at once. After a few moments, the pain subsided and I realized, Shane was breathing harshly and was staring at me with a mixture of desire and worry in his eyes. Belatedly I realized he was also speaking to me in my head. However, his voice sounded like a whisper.

"Lela? Are you ok?"

"I'm fine, Shane," I thought back arching against him instinctively. His hips thrust into me automatically and he groaned. *"Jordan and the crew were all talking in my head at once and it overwhelmed me. You aren't hurting me."*

I had been in pain from all of them talking in my head, but Shane clearly hadn't known he wasn't the cause. Luckily our suspect wouldn't know that either.

I could feel that Shane had taken just about all of the excitement he could handle. His concern had quickly transformed into something more primal. He was clearly fighting desire now that he knew I wasn't hurt. I began to move against him to push him over the edge. I was ready for this to end. His body jerked automatically every time I rubbed against his now very rigid erection. I tried to make my movements appear to be a struggle, albeit, a very weak one. If I was being honest with myself, feeling Shane so intimately pressing against me was turning me on with every movement of our bodies.

Unfortunately, through all of the distraction of Jordan losing it, the others talking in my head and causing me to see stars, and Shane now biting me gently on my neck as our bodies jerked together, I'd lost track of the drainer. I only had time to scream Shane's name in his head as the thought came to me, breaking through my haze of sensations. I realized too late that Shane's hand was still around my neck. Our suspect thought I was going limp from oxygen deprivation and passing out.

"He's killing her. I have to do something," he was thinking just as he flew at Shane like lighting and slammed into him. Shane was a little awkward and took another blow before he finally got his wits about him and flung his assailant off of him. The kid, for

it was a kid, looked a little surprised and wary. He hesitated, for the briefest moment trying to understand how Shane was able to throw him off so easily before his survival instinct kicked in and he turned to run.

Luckily, Logan and crew saw the kid coming and had begun to move the moment they saw the kid coming after Shane. Logan and Ethan had the kid trussed up before he'd had a chance to take two steps. Jordan, on the other hand, completely bypassed the kid and dealt Shane a blow that sat him flat on his ass.

"Jordan!" I yelled as Jordan stood heaving over Shane with wrath in his eyes. Shane made no move to get up or retaliate. Daisy and Grace made it there before I did and put themselves between the two men.

"What the hell are you doing?" I thundered at Jordan. His chest was heaving with unleased fury as he glared down at Shane. How was I going to defuse this? But this time it was the calm voice of Logan that reined Jordan in.

"Jordan, get a hold of yourself," he began calmly, but there was steel in his voice. "Lela is fine. She and Shane have done nothing but the job they were asked to do."

He looked at me then and I couldn't read what was in his eyes. The emotions were so deep and varied, I didn't dare open my senses. I was barely on my feet as it as. My whole body was trembling with fatigue, arousal, and probably shock.

"Grace, Ethan, Jordan, and I have to get this suspect to the facility. You take Lela home," he commanded Daisy.

"I can drive myself," I retorted. I snatched back the restraining hand I had put on Jordan's arm and stepped over to Shane.

"I'm fine," he said waving me away before I could bend down in front of him. He didn't appear mad, but I couldn't read his face. I was done reading minds for the night, so I didn't bother trying.

"I'll ride with you," Jordan finally spoke behind me, but I didn't look at him.

"No. You won't." Logan's voice was uncompromising as he glared at his brother. Then, he turned to Shane. "Are you alright, Shane?"

"I'm fine, Logan," Shane replied never taking his eyes from Jordan as he rubbed his jaw where Jordan had punched him. Other than the fact that he seemed a little shaken, he didn't appear to be any worse for wear.

"Good. Drive your car back to the ranch," Logan ordered. "We'll meet you there."

"Ok," he replied slowly getting to his feet. His calm demeanor never changed, though I knew there was something going on behind that calm facade. My head, however, still ached some from the bombardment and all of the mind reading I'd been doing, so I didn't think I could handle listening in.

"I don't want you driving, Lela," Logan insisted. "Daisy will drive you home. You can change clothes and meet us back at the ranch."

I nodded and began walking back to Blake's car. I didn't turn to see if Daisy followed, but she was soon walking quietly beside me.

Chapter 20

I arrived at the ranch two hours later. I was cleaned up and dressed in my usual jeans and a t-shirt with a healthy dose of my own furry. I knew I would be the walking dead tomorrow but, at the moment, I didn't feel any fatigue. I wanted to get this interrogation over with, and I wanted to finally get Jordan to myself so that I could let him have it. I reminded myself that for now, I had to put my anger on the back burner and put my professional face front and center.

Once I arrived, Daisy ushered me into the same room where I'd listened to Agnes' interview. I noticed Shane was absent and my anger grew. I'd have to call Shane and make things right.

My anger at Jordan and his high handed behavior vanished once I opened my senses to the boy in the other room with Ethan and Logan. He was terrified and wasn't talking at all. Ethan and Logan were not being overly forceful with the kid, but the kid didn't trust them. So far they didn't even know is name.

"They're going to kill me anyway. What difference does it make who I am?" was one of the jumbled thoughts going through his mind. *"But, why do they have healers here. Are healers working with them now?"*

"Look, it's late. And you look like you are tired and hungry," Ethan was saying, trying not to sound frustrated. "Why don't you at least tell us your name?"

The kid was completely ignoring them and trying to scent everything around the room. He wanted to figure out where he was and use any possibility to escape. He wasn't going down without a fight.

"He thinks you guys are planning to kill him," I thought to Logan and then Ethan.

"Why would we want to kill him?" Logan thought back.

"I'm not sure. His thoughts are all over the place," I thought back. *"He's afraid, terrified actually. I'm getting the sense that something happened to him. He's running from someone. And, he thinks you are it."*

A moment later, Logan was telling Ethan to watch the kid and he'd be right back. Then Logan came striding through the door to the office where the rest of us were seated.

"Ok. I'm at a total loss here," Logan thought to me as he came to stand in front of me and gave a helpless shrug.

"I don't think you and Ethan are going to get much out of him. I think maybe us girls should try," I suggested.

159

Everyone was swiveling their heads back and forth as Logan and I gestured to each other through our silent conversation.

"*This guy, this kid, is a murderer,*" Logan was thinking.

"*Yes, but he was only murdering people who were hurting someone else. I think it triggers a sense of helplessness in him for not being able to protect himself and others,*" I thought as my hands gestured. "*There's something deeper here. He's not a cold hearted, crazed killer. And, he thinks you are possibly what he's been running from. He's determined not to respond to you.*"

"*Fine. Daisy and Grace can do it. But, they don't normally do interrogations and interviews,*" Logan thought, giving in grudgingly.

"*I'm going in too,*" I demanded.

"*Lela, don't you think Jordan has been through enough tonight,*" he gave me a pointed look. I narrowed my eyes at him.

"*Jordan? What does he have to do with this?*" I practically shouted in his head. He put his hands up in a surrender gesture and turned to the rest of the room.

"Listen up. We all need to meet in my office right now," he said to the rest of the room before turning his thoughts back to me. "*It's the only room in the house that's sound proof where you can explain your wild idea to everyone else.*"

I guess he didn't know that Jordan had told me about his and Grace's sound proof bedroom, I thought absently. Everyone

160

quickly filed out of the room, eager to find out what was going on. Logan stopped in and told Ethan he'd be back in a moment.

Once we were all crammed into Logan's office, he closed the door and turned to the cramped room.

"From what Lela has been able to pick up, our suspect is determined not to talk to us. Apparently, he's afraid and thinks we are planning to kill him," he began.

"Kill him? Why?" Daisy asked.

"I'm not sure. Something happened to him," I said and proceeded to tell them the same things I'd already told Logan.

"Lela suggests you ladies take a stab at it. He clearly doesn't trust drainers. He's uncertain and suspicious about the healers, but not like he is about us drainers," Logan explained. "So you guys have a better chance of getting something out of him."

"And, my presence should definitely tip the scales in our favor," I added. Jordan shot up out of his chair.

"Jordan, either get a grip or get the hell out of here," Logan said angrily. The brothers glared at each other for a moment, and then Jordan turned and walked from the room. The tension in the room was thick and palpable.

"He's already confused about why drainers and healers are together," I continued, not acknowledging Jordan's departure. "So, I guess that is as unusual as you say outside of the Alexander clan. But, having a regular person like myself there, and unharmed by drainers, might help."

"Or he might just feel like you set him up and not trust you," Grace said thoughtfully.

"That is a possibility. I guess we will see," Logan said. "Now let's back in there. Ethan and I will stay in the room with you, but we'll stay in the background."

"But, we don't usually do interrogations," Daisy stated doubtfully.

"You've seen enough of them. You can handle this," Logan assured her. "We need to know his name, who he is, and why he's killing people."

I'd never seen Logan so on the edge. He was staying calm, but it was clear that he was close to the end of his rope as well.

"I also suggest we get the kid some food. He's hungry. That may also make him more agreeable, if we can get him to eat," I suggested.

"I'll grab an unopened bag of chips and a can of soda," Daisy volunteered. "That way he can see me open it in front of him and not be afraid we are trying to poison him."

"Good thinking, Daze," Grace smiled.

With that, we headed back to the room where Ethan was keeping watch over the kid. When we walked in, the kid went from suspiciously watching Ethan's every move to a look of total panic and confusion. Daisy rushed in with two bags of potato chips and several sodas just as we were taking our seats. I kept forgetting just how fast they could move. I guessed the slow pace, or normal pace, to and from Logan's office was for my benefit. I took my seat as Daisy took a seat next to me. Ethan closed the door behind her.

"My name is Grace, and I am a doctor," Grace began in a light voice. Then she gestured to each of us in turn. "This is Daisy, Ethan, Logan and Lela. No one here is going to hurt you."

"B-But, you're a healer. And, so is she," he said uncertainly pointing to Daisy.

"That's right. We are both healers," she nodded and smiled a motherly smile.

"But, they're drainers," the boy blurted out in confusion. "Drainers don't hang out with healers."

"Actually, the one there," she said pointing at Logan, "he's my husband. You are right though. It's not a normal thing."

His eyes widened in disbelief and then he frowned in suspicion. He wasn't sure if she was lying or not. Then he turned his eyes to me. "And you are just a regular old person."

"Well, I'm not really that old," I said feeling strange at being called old. I was only twenty-two after all. "But, you are right again. I am only a normal human. How old are you?"

Looking at the kid now, I judged him to be no more than fifteen. He was a big kid for his age, tall and lean. He was as big as a man. But, there was something so innocent about his face that I didn't think he was as old as his body might suggest.

"Drainers kill people," he said ignoring my question.

"Is that why you killed those men?" Daisy asked casually.

"No. I killed them because they were hurting those women. Those women don't seem to know that they shouldn't be out there late at night like that. And, no one was there to protect them," he said sounding defensive and confused. I couldn't help but think he was way too sheltered.

Daisy opened up a bag of chips and offered them casually to Grace and me. We each took a few chips and munched on them as Grace asked the next question.

"So, you were there to protect them?" she asked. I watched his eyes follow the bag. He was intently focused on every chew that we made.

"Well, yea," he said still focusing on the chips. And hunger ripped through me as he thought about his own hunger.

"Ethan will you pass me a tissue?" I asked.

Ethan grabbed the box of tissue off of the desk and handed it to me. I pulled several tissues from the box and placed them in front of each of us. Then, I poured out some chips for Daisy, Grace, and myself.

"Would you like some chips…uh," I hesitated. "I'm sorry, I don't know your name."

"Gerald," the boy said absently as he stared at the chips.

"Would you like some chips Gerald?" I asked lightly. He swallowed visibly.

"Yes, please," he said never taking his eyes off the bag. I spread a few of the tissues out in front of him and poured out a large pile of chips. I was half worried that he might accidently eat the tissue in his haste to consume the chips. I looked over at Daisy and Grace to find them looking sympathetically at Gerald.

"How old are you, Gerald?" I asked while he was devouring the chips. I caught Daisy's eye and nodded towards the soda.

"Twelve," Gerald said with a mouth full of chips. That took everyone by surprise, but Gerald didn't seem to notice.

"Would you like a soda, Gerald," Daisy asked regaining her composure. He looked up and eyed her and the can suspiciously for a moment.

"It's unopened. Would you like me to open it for you?" Daisy asked. Listening to his mind, I knew Daisy had obviously been able pick up on his thoughts or make an accurate guess without my help. He was definitely still suspicious, though his hunger and the proximity of food were distracting him and making him careless.

"I can open it," he said but made no move to take the can. Daisy slid it in front of him. He eyed it for a moment and then popped the top. He took a long swallow and then dove back into the chips.

"Where are your parents?" Grace asked softly. He looked up now and stared at her.

"Dead," he said when he finally spoke and swallowed hard. He looked so young and devastated then.

A flood of images entered his head. He was in a barn removing tack from a horse. Shots were fired some distance away and then he was running towards a house. The scenes were coming so fast, I couldn't make sense of them all. In the next scene he was standing in a room of horror. There was blood everywhere and a woman lay face down on the carpet. There appeared to be a body partially hidden by the sofa. The name Arthur flitted through his mind before the image of a man with a gun flashed through his mind. There was a feeling of fear and anguish. Then, the image blurred as he seemed to turn and run. I sucked in a deep breath and tried to cover it with a cough. He looked at me sharply.

"What happened to your parents?" Ethan asked.

"They were killed by drainers," Gerald stated flatly.

"Wait a minute?" I said trying to act as though I was recovering from my cough. I had just discovered something. I just had no idea what it was. "Are you from that family that was killed?"

His eyes became huge, "You know my family?"

"No. I just heard about a family that had been killed or something. I don't know if it was a home invasion or what," I improvised. Honestly, I hadn't heard anything, nor did I know anything about what had happened to him or his family. I could feel everyone's eyes on me. I was sure hoping they knew something about this, because I didn't know anything else. Luckily Logan saved me.

"Wait, are you talking about that family near Pacifica? But, I heard the whole family was murdered," Logan chimed in.

"Not everyone," Gerald said angrily. "I was the only one who survived."

Logan and Ethan moved in closer.

"Gerald, have you ever heard of Alexander Ranch?" Logan asked.

"Yes. My parents said that they investigate bad drainers and capture them," he looked down at the table. "I mean that's what they used to say."

"Do you know where you are, Gerald?" Grace asked tilting her head to the side. He shook his head but didn't look up. Grace looked at me and I shook my head to indicate that he didn't have any idea. He was currently wallowing in grief and thoughts of his parents and Arthur. There was an image of a younger boy in his head.

"I am Logan Alexander, Gerald. You are at Alexander Ranch right now," Logan said looking at the boy closely. His head snapped up and fear crossed his face.

"I didn't really mean to kill those men," he blurted out. "I was just so angry. And, when I started to hit them I just couldn't stop."

He looked on the verge of tears.

"It's ok, Gerald. You're safe now. No one is blaming you, I broke in before anyone could respond. I saw Logan bristle a little but he didn't say anything. "We just want to know what happened and to help you."

"He's telling the truth, Logan," I thought to Logan hastily. *"From what I can tell, he is suffering from a great deal of grief and guilt at not being able to protect his family. He's taking out the aggression he wishes he could have taken out on the people who killed his family on these other men who are hurting people. It's like transference. He couldn't save his family. He feels guilty for running when the men realized they'd missed someone and came after him. So, he's trying to assuage his own guilt by saving others."*

"She's right," Logan said a bit stiffly. "We just need to know what happened so we know how to protect you."

Gerald paused and looked around for a moment. Then the damn of his pent up anger, frustration and pain broke. The story came flooding out of him. He'd been out riding. He hadn't even known anything was wrong until he'd been in the barn removing his horse's tack. He'd heard shots and ran as fast as he could. And then he'd walked in on the scene I'd already seen in his head. He'd been desperate to find his little brother once he knew he couldn't help his parents. But, a man had come out of nowhere and pointed a gun at him. He'd turned and fled. He wasn't sure why the man hadn't caught him. Something must have delayed the man. By the time the man had come after him, he'd taken off and headed to the beach and into the water where they wouldn't be able to track his scent.

It was heartbreaking for me. Not only to hear his words, but to see the visions in his mind and feel all the emotions he was going through, knowing he was telling us nothing but the truth. This poor kid had lived through so much in just under a month. He was not a monster, or even vicious, yet he'd killed several men. The abyss of his hurt and pain, and having no one to help him even survive, no place to live, everything he'd known and loved ripped from him, definitely caused him to crack and do things he would never have done under normal circumstances. Tears leaked from his eyes and he dashed them away angrily, not wanting to appear weak by crying.

"Gerald, what you have been through is horrible. I can't begin to imagine how hard this must have been for you," I said, trying to hold back my own tears. I shut down my senses. So far he was telling us the complete, heart wrenching truth as he knew it. Staying in his head would do nothing more then drain my energy and emotions down further. I'd picked up enough to have a few things I wanted to question him about.

He felt such extreme remorse over not being able to help his parents. He wasn't even sure if they were dead when he'd found them. He was holding in extreme amounts of guilt in not knowing. If they hadn't been dead yet, he could have probably saved them, or found a healer that would do it. His parents had been acquainted with a few healers. Since, his family did not harm people, they'd never had any problems with the local healers. They'd kept to themselves and were always cordial with the healers they encountered.

Another one of his emotionally bleeding wounds was caused by someone named Arthur. I had gotten the impression when I was in his head that this may have been a younger sibling. He was barely coherent whenever he thought of this Arthur. The pain that shot through him was crippling to me whenever he had thought of this kid. Arthur was a younger child who was not dark haired like Gerald. He had rich reddish brown hair and Green eyes flecked with golds and browns. He was a striking little kid from what I could tell in Gerald's mind. And, Gerald was sick at not knowing what had happened to him, yet feeling certain that he was also dead. Gerald had not been able to save him either.

"Gerald, do you have any idea who these people are that killed your parents? Any idea who would want to hurt your parents?" I asked, working my way up to the question of Arthur.

Gerald shook his head. "No. We kept to ourselves. We didn't bother anyone. I don't understand."

I could feel all eyes on me as Logan and Ethan allowed me to take the lead on the questioning for the moment.

"So, are you an only child?" I asked cautiously, re-opening my senses and trying to be prepared for whatever response he had that might slam into me. "You are the only survivor of what happened to your family?"

"No. I mean, yes," he stammered trying to hold back tears. He paused to take a deep breath and then spoke again. "I have…, had a little brother. He's dead too. Only, I don't know what happened to him."

A very disturbing suspicion was starting to form in my mind. I glanced over at Logan and, with my senses still opened, could feel the same suspicion forming in his mind. It was likely forming in everyone's mind, but I didn't check. I was already exhausted enough.

I'd obviously built up some endurance with my mind reading abilities since I began working with the Alexanders and using my gift. Originally, I couldn't last very long. After much shorter periods of time than I had been using it lately, using my ability wore me completely out. I'd never kept it up for this long, and I was beginning to buckle under the shear strain of it. The emotional strain was also not helping much.

"How do you know for certain that Arthur is dead?" I asked.

"He's just a kid." Gerald paused realizing again he'd spoken of his brother in the present tense. "There's no way he could have survived. He was only eight. When I left to go ride my horse that morning, he was sitting in the family room watching television with my parents. They were all still there in the family room when I ran in after hearing the gun shots. Only, there was blood everywhere, and I could see my mother lying in her own blood on the carpet-"

"So, you actually saw Arthur?" I asked cutting him off. I could see the image in his mind and I just couldn't take anymore. I didn't want to hear the details of what he saw or go through it in his head with him."

"Well, no," he said frowning. His mind went blessedly blank with confusion at my question. "I never saw him, but he was there."

"Gerald, we think that there is a possibility your brother is still alive," Logan said taking over the interview. Gerald's head snapped up to Logan's.

"But..., how? I mean, why...? I don't understand," he said looking from Logan to me.

"If you can come with us and verify whether or not you recognize your brother's scent or not, we will be able to answer your question," Logan said recapturing his attention.

"You know where my brother is? You've seen him?" he asked anxiously.

"No, we don't know for sure where he is, or even if the scent belongs to your brother," Logan answered quickly. "But, if it is your brother's scent, then we know he's still alive as of yesterday. And, we should be able to help you find him."

"Well, let's go," Gerald said jumping to his feet so fast I didn't see the movement. One minute he was in the chair. The next second he was on his feet.

"Are you up to going to the morgue with us? I know you said he's telling the truth, but I'm more concerned with how he reacts when he finds out his brothers been killing dogs and women," Logan thought to me. I turned to look at him and then everyone else in the room. Everyone had varying degrees of concern on their faces, however, everyone but Logan's was focused on Gerald. *"I'm really confused here. This kid doesn't seem like a cold blooded killer, so I'm suspecting that his brother isn't either. That leaves me with no explanation as to why he's killing these women. If Gerald has a clue to what's going on with his brother, I want to know about it."*

Chapter 21

It was well past two in the morning when we arrived at the morgue with Grace. Logan hadn't wanted an entourage so it was only him, Grace, Gerald and me. Jordan hadn't been anywhere to be seen when we walked out of the little office where we'd been feeding and questioning Gerald.

Gerald seemed a bit confused when he realized we were entering the morgue. His eyes widened and he stopped dead in his tracks. I didn't need to open my senses to realize what he was thinking.

"Gerald, your brother is not here," I said turning to face him and looking directly into his wild eyes. "We didn't bring you here to identify your brother, only his scent. We think he may have been in contact with someone who died in the last 48 hours."

Relief briefly flittered over Gerald's features and his tensed muscles began to relax before a frown of confusion and wariness formed on his young face. Logan nudged him forward gently and he began walking again, hesitantly. We continued down the hall and entered an exam like room. The moment Grace pulled open one of the freezer like doors and pulled the table holding a body out, Gerald began to scent the air and his eyes popped with shocked recognition. He hurried over to the body and stared down at it.

"Who is she?" he asked turning to Grace.

"Her name is Alissa James," Grace answered evenly. "Do you smell your brother's scent with hers?"

"Yes. But, why would his scent be with this dead woman's? I've never seen her before. He couldn't have known her."

"Gerald," Logan said putting his hand on Gerald's shoulder. "Do you notice that she's been drained?"

Gerald went pale. He turned back to the woman and then back to Logan.

"Are…, are you saying…that," he swallowed and tried again, "that, Arthur did this?"

"We think he may have," Logan nodded. "Did you notice, though, that she was drained very, uh, gently? She was not drained the way the men you killed were drained. Do you have any idea why Arthur might do this?"

Gerald stiffened. "Arthur wouldn't do this. If you want to put me in jail for killing those men, I'll go. But, Arthur wouldn't do this. He wouldn't kill anyone."

Gerald believed what he was saying. He could not comprehend that his brother would kill anyone. He was baffled over the whole thing and now scared for his little brother. I thought it best that Logan didn't tell him about the other victims just yet. That might be counterproductive at this point. So, I thought my thoughts directly to Logan and then to Grace.

"I'm sure you can tell that this woman was drained, and we don't have the scent of any other drainer than Arthur," Logan said seeming to find it hard to get the words out. "But, the way that she was drained might mean it was an accident."

"Maybe, he hadn't eaten and didn't realize he was draining her too much," Gerald said grabbing on to the possible explanation. "But, where is he now? How do we find him?"

"Unfortunately, we aren't likely to locate him until tomorrow night, or rather," he looked at his watch, "tonight. We'll need you to be with us. We've caught his scent in roughly the same location at night, but he also caught ours and ran."

Gerald nodded at this in understanding. After all, he'd done the same thing when he'd caught the scent of the drainers and healers together.

"But, what if he's still there?" he asked in agitation.

"He's not. We've had a team out searching for his scent. He's long gone," Logan assured him. "He's also very good at covering his scent to prevent being tracked."

"So, what do we do then? Just leave him out there?" Gerald cried. "He's afraid of the dark. He's got to be terrified."

"I know this is hard. But, we are going to take you there tonight hoping to make sure he catches your scent. After catching your scent, he'll hopefully come out of hiding if he knows you are there," Logan explained. "So, as hard as this is, I'm going to need you to hang on until tonight. Ok?"

Gerald nodded gravely.

"Right now, we are going to get you cleaned up and fed. Then, we need you to try and get some rest so you'll be ready to help us find your brother tonight," Logan continued. "It's only a few hours from now."

"Ok. I can do that," Gerald nodded again. "But, will you promise you won't put my brother in jail?"

"Gerald, if your brother is as innocent as you say he is, then there is no reason he should go to jail," Logan said neatly sidestepping the question. It worked. Gerald was just that sure that his brother couldn't have possibly killed that woman on purpose.

Chapter 22

"Lela, I can't tell you how much you've helped tonight," Logan said once we were back at the ranch and in his office. Grace had taken Gerald away and was having him tended to. The rest of the crew was waiting to be debriefed, but Logan had asked to speak to me in his office.

"I didn't really do much, Logan," I shrugged.

"Lela? Yes, you did," he said sounding incredulous. "You really don't see how much time you saved us by asking the right questions at the right times based on what things you were able to gain from his thoughts? It may not seem like much to you, but it really is. I mean, how would we have gotten to the question of his brother?"

I could see his point. He would have likely gotten to it eventually, but I was too tired to want to even discuss it.

"Anyway, I can see you are exhausted. Please take the day off tomorrow," he said. A bit of his commanding tone had entered his voice. "I can call John tomorrow and tell him we need you tomorrow if necessary."

"No, Logan. I appreciate it. But, I'll just take a vacation day. I don't want you to do that," I answered.

"And, I don't want you using your vacation time," he said and sighed. "That brings me to something else I need to talk to you about, but it will have to wait until after this mess is over with Gerald and his brother. We'll need you to go with us tomorrow night. Are you sure you don't want to stay here in one of the guest rooms?"

"No. I'm fine," I insisted. I didn't want to be anywhere near Jordan tonight and he definitely wouldn't be staying at my place. If I was here, it would be much harder to get rid of him.

"Ok. I'll have Jordan drive you home," he said shaking his head with a smile. "Go home and get some rest."

I didn't want Jordan to drive me home either. But, if that was the fastest way I could get to my own house and have some solitude, I'd just have to grin and bear it a little longer. When Logan and I walked out of his office, Jordan was waiting for us. I didn't bother to look at him. I just headed for the front door as I heard Logan telling him to take me home. I walked out the front door. Soon, Jordan fell into step beside me and opened the passenger side door for me.

The ride home was deathly quiet and full of tension. Once we finally arrived at my house, I jumped out of the car and practically sprinted to the front door. Jordan still made it to the front door at the same time I did. I opened the front door with my key, turned the security alarm off, and turned to him.

"Thank you for driving me home. I'll see you tomorrow," I said pointedly.

"I'm not leaving, Lela."

"Yes, Jordan, you are," I said firmly.

"Then, I'll leave in a few minutes, after we've talked," he said clenching his jaw.

"Jordan, it's past three in the morning. I've been up for almost twenty-four hours and I didn't have much sleep to begin with. We can talk tomorrow."

"Are you mad at me?" he asked narrowing his eyes.

"We can talk about it tomorrow," I repeated impatiently.

"You can't even just answer a question now," he growled. Oh, this really pricked my ire.

"Yes, Jordan!" I snapped. "I'm mad at you. Did you really think Shane would hurt me?"

"No. I mean it was very hard to watch him slamming you around like that. And, yes, I had a moment of panic when he grabbed you by the hair. I mean, that was not necessary. That was a bit too rough."

"No, it wasn't. We've practiced that. A real attacker would do that. Shane makes sure I'm ready for anything. Now, goodnight!"

"What the hell are you mad at me for?"

He actually looked confused.

"Well, if you don't know, I 'm not about to explain it to you now," I said throwing my hands in the air.

"Let me get this straight," Jordan said taking the few steps towards me to get close enough to bend down right into my face.

"You were the one being dry humped against a wall with Shane's hands all over you, yet you are mad at me?"

"He was supposed to have his hands all over me!" I shouted in disbelieving frustration. "He was doing his job! First you get in front of everyone and try to dictate to me what I can and cannot do. Now you're punching people? What the hell is this, Jordan?"

"Oh, I think he was doing a bit more than his job," Jordan shot back. I frowned at him in total bafflement.

"Jordan, I was posing as a hooker. He was posing as a jon," I gritted out poking him in the chest. "It wasn't like he was groping me or something."

"He ripped your shirt practically off! And.., and-" he said gesturing wildly.

"That's why I had the tank top under it," I spat out, my hands gesturing wildly. I was fuming and full of indignation and frustration. "This is exactly why Grace and Logan didn't want you there, Jordan. This is ridiculous. And then you punched him! You had no right to hit him. Thankfully, Shane kept his calm, otherwise it would have turned into a brawl."

"I know lust when I see it, Lela," he snarled down at me. "Yours and his. So don't try to defend him. I don't want him anywhere near you. Do you hear me?"

I reared back as if he'd slapped me. I just stood there speechless. Yes, I'd felt Shane's erection pressing into me at the end there. And, of course I knew that Shane was attracted to me. But, I'm sure he wouldn't have had that reaction with everyone there if he could have helped it. Considering the circumstances, I thought he handled things quite well. And, yes, I will freely admit that I had my own physical reaction to Shane. He's an attractive guy. What girl wouldn't have a reaction to such intimate contact, especially knowing that he would never hurt me? But, lust? I was certainly not lusting after Shane. And, I honestly didn't think he was lusting after me.

"What exactly are you trying to accuse me of?" I asked with dangerous calm.

"I'm stating the facts. I know what I saw. And, all you have done is defend him. Why exactly is that, Lela?" he asked with his own tone of menace.

"Get out, Jordan," I said stepping past him and opening the door.

"So, you *aren't* denying whatever is going on between the two of you?" he asked knowingly. A distasteful expression settled on his face.

"Whatever is going on between Shane and me is all in your head. So no. I'm not going to sit here and defend myself for doing the job I was asked to do. And, I'm sure as hell not going to sit here and listen to you try to order me around and tell me who I can and cannot be around. Now get out!" I yelled.

"Fine!" he roared with eyes blazing. He turned and was out the door. I tried to take the door off the hinges slamming it in frustration behind him. How dare he accuse me! I was vibrating with rage and hurt. Under the circumstance, I don't think either Shane or I could have found it exactly lust inducing, regardless of our slight physical reactions. At best it was stressful. The only comfort was having Shane there and knowing that he and the others would keep me safe should some real nut job, or even just a strange man, come a calling.

I locked up and headed for my bathroom, stripping angrily the whole way. By the time I stepped in and the water began to lightly beat my body from the spray, I was crying from all of the mental pain, frustration, emotions and fatigue I'd held at bay. Yes, I'd showered earlier, then again after the undercover operation I'd been asked to play a part in, and before I met with the Alexander's at the ranch. But, I would have a hard enough time sleeping now. I was too tired to sleep, too wound up to relax, and too upset to find peace. After hastily finishing the shower and donning a nightgown, I crawled under my covers feeling like I couldn't possibly go one step further. Luckily, I feel asleep within minutes.

I awoke to the muffled sound of my cell phone ringing, somewhere. I ignored it. But, just as I was dozing off the house phone rang. I had one of the cordless phones right next to my bed, so when it began to ring there was no ignoring it.

"Yes?" I answered, my voice sounding croaky with the lack of use and emotional strain of weeping from the night before.

"Lela?" Daisy asked tentatively. "Did I wake you up?"

"Uh, yea," I said rolling over to look at my clock. I was startled to find that it was after one o'clock in the afternoon. Considering that it was after three when I finally went to bed, that shouldn't be so shocking. It was only about ten hours of much needed sleep. But, considering I would usually wake up no later than about eight in the morning no matter what time I went to bed, it was a testament to how exhausted I really was that I'd slept that long.

"I'm sorry," she said hesitantly. "I just wanted to check on you and see how you were. Do you want some company, or would you rather be alone? I'm off right now until tonight. So, I was planning to stop by if it was ok with you."

Actually, I wouldn't mind company right now. I didn't want to start wallowing again, and I could feel the heaviness of the past twenty-four hours beginning to weigh on me.

"Actually, I wouldn't mind some company," I said trying to sound cheerful. "I'll leave the door open for you."

"That sounds good," Daisy chuckled. "I'm already standing on your porch."

Sure enough, when I dragged myself out of bed, made my way to the front door and pulled it open, Daisy was right there with a big smile on her face.

"Hey," I said pulling the cordless phone from my ear and hitting the off button. I opened the door wide in greeting and made my way back to my bed. Daisy closed the door behind herself and followed me to my room. She flopped down on my bed next to me. I half expected her to wrinkle her nose, sensing Jordan's smell on my bed, but she didn't.

"How are you today?" she asked.

"I'm fine," I answered briskly. She sighed.

"I guess that means you don't want to talk about it?" she asked.

"Nothing to talk about," I retorted with my eyes closed.

"I figured as much," Daisy said sounding as if she were holding on to her patience. "Well then just listen. I have a pretty good idea that Jordan didn't handle things very well last night. He wasn't handling them well when I was around, so I can only imagine how he acted once the two of you arrived here last night."

"Yea, he accused me of…, well, I'm not sure exactly. But, apparently there is something going on with Shane and me according to Jordan," I said opening my eyes to look at her as I spoke. She flinched.

"Yea, I kind of figured he'd do something dumb like that." Daisy shook her head. "Well, I have no excuse for him. I mean, it was really hard to watch. I've never seen Shane appear so menacing, and you really looked scared. I just had to keep telling myself that Shane wouldn't hurt you or anyone else."

"No he wouldn't. Though, I almost think Jordan would have appreciated that more. He said something along the lines of recognizing an apparent lust Shane and I have for each other," I explained blandly.

"Oh, Jordan," Daisy mumbled to herself rolling her eyes. "He can be an idiot sometimes, can't he?"

"So, what was your impression," I asked watching her closely. She turned and met my eyes.

"I thought you guys did a very convincing job," Daisy stated firmly. "It was pretty rough to watch."

"So, it didn't look *lustful* to you?" I asked sarcastically.

"No," Daisy said waving her hand in a dismissive gesture before continuing. "I'll be blunt. Did I notice Shane had gotten a little aroused rubbing against you the way he was? Yes. But, I can't imagine most guys being able to pull that off without having some sort of reaction. Honestly, that was one of the only things that helped me remember it was all an act. I just don't believe Shane could get, well, aroused actually trying to hurt anyone. I couldn't tell exactly how you were reacting to Shane though. But regardless, I know that the scene I saw was not one of simple lust."

"Thanks, Daisy," I said with my throat feeling a bit tight. I needed to hear that.

"Don't worry about it," she said patting my arm. "Once Jordan calms down, his rational side will kick in and he'll begin acting normal again."

"I don't care about his rational side, or any other side. I don't think I can do this. First, he's trying to tell me what I can and cannot do in front of all of you. Now, he's getting jealous, or something, punching people for doing their jobs, and accusing me of having something going with Shane. This is too much. I can't do this. Clearly, I'm not cut out for relationships."

"Oh," Daisy said studying me with astonishment. "He must have really acted an ass last night."

"You know Daisy, I really don't want to talk about it," I said and reclosed my eyes.

"Alright then. On to the next topic," she said without missing a beat. "Have you eaten anything?"

"No. I just woke up when you called, remember?"

"Yes. I remember," she smiled. "How about I run and bring us something to eat. You don't look like you are up for going out."

"I'm not."

"Right," Daisy said and stood. "How about I run and pick up some Thai food and meet you back here."

"Sounds good."

Daisy hadn't been out the door for two minutes before my cell phone was ringing again. I got up and found where the muffled sound was coming from. It was in my purse. I dug around in my purse to see that Ethan was calling me.

"Hi, Ethan," I said trying to sound jovial.

"Hey, sweetheart. How are you?"

"I'm good," I assured him.

"Are you sure? You sure you don't want me and Logan to take Jordan out back and beat on him a little?"

"That's not necessary," I chuckled.

"Do you want me to come over?" he asked.

"You are welcome to. Daisy just left to go get Thai food. Give her a call and tell her to pick up some extra," I suggested.

"I'm on it. I'll see you in just a few minutes."

As soon as I hung up with Ethan, my phone rang again as I was heading for the kitchen to make coffee. It was Shane. What was this? Where they tag teaming me?

"Hi Shane," I said smiling. I'd been embarrassed at Jordan's punching him yesterday. I'd wanted to talk to him but wasn't sure if he wanted to talk to me.

"Hey, Lela," he said in that easy voice of his. "How are you today?"

"I'm fine. How are *you* doing today?"

"I'm fine, really," he said dismissively. "I just wanted to make sure you were ok. I know Jordan was really pissed last night."

"I am so sorry for that," I said sincerely, feeling embarrassed all over again. "He had no right or reason to hit you like that."

"Don't be too hard on him." Shane sounded a little uncomfortable himself.

"I didn't think I was being hard on him at all," I answered not understanding. "He was the one having fits and punching people."

"He didn't hurt me, Lela. And," he hesitated, "don't take this the wrong way, but I'm not so sure if it were the other way around that I wouldn't have punched him."

Now what was I supposed to say to that? What was that supposed to even mean?

"Lela?"

"I'm here."

"This is embarrassing," he said sounding like he'd rather be cutting his tongue out. "I'm just saying that it's no secret that I am attracted to you. And, obviously since he found us kissing a while back he's aware of it too."

"Yes, but he and I weren't even together then," I interrupted.

"Doesn't matter. You know that I would never do anything to get in between your relationship with Jordan. But, that doesn't mean it was easy for him to watch what he did last night."

"So, what? You are calling me to tell me not to be mad at him?" I asked.

"Well, no. That wasn't the reason I called," he admitted. "I just wanted to make sure you were alright. Last night couldn't have been easy for you either."

"No. It wasn't."

"So, you're good?"

"I'm good, Shane."

"Ok, well you know you can call me if you need to right?" he asked.

"Yes. And thank you."

"No problem. I'm sure Jordan can't stay upset too long," he said. "In the meantime, I think it's probably not a good idea to have our sparring sessions."

"What? Why not? Did Jordan say something to you?" I asked getting angry all over again.

"I haven't talked to Jordan," he said sounding confused. "I'm pretty sure I am the last person he wants to talk to or see right now."

"He's an ass," I snarled. "And, thank you for not retaliating. That would have been pretty ugly if you guys had started brawling in the street."

"Just give him a few days, Lela," he coaxed. "Like I said, I can understand why he was upset. No need for me to make it worse by giving him the fight he wanted."

"You are just way too noble," I accused. He laughed.

"No. I'm not. I just don't want any fighting or anything over this," he said. "You know what you want. It would hardly make sense for me to be fighting a losing battle over you."

I didn't want to read too much into that, but I was at a complete loss for a response to that.

"Anyway, I'd better let you go," Shane said into the silence. "I was just on my way out."

"Ok." I answered dumbly.

"Bye, Lela."

"Bye, Shane."

By the time Ethan and Daisy arrived at my house with food, I was finishing up my now afternoon coffee. Ethan had apparently caught up with her because they arrived together. The day ended up being quite fun with Daisy and Ethan there ensconced in my family room with me watching the television. I was sort of sad to see the day end. It had probably been the most relaxing day I'd had since I'd arrived home from my vacation. The way I was currently feeling, another vacation was looking pretty good.

"We have to head out soon," Daisy said to Ethan around seven in the evening. She stood and looked at him expectantly. He turned to me.

"Logan doesn't want you there for the take down-" Ethan began.

"I'm coming," I replied. No one attempted to argue. I ran and threw on some jeans and combed my hair.

We headed out a little before eight to meet up with the others. Tonight it was just Grace, Logan, Jordan, Gerald and myself. Ethan, Daisy and Shane were apparently assigned to do something else. I wasn't sure why Jordan was needed but didn't ask.

"This is where my brother is?" Gerald asked doubtfully looking at the depressing surroundings.

"Well, this is one place we know he has been coming recently," Logan answered. "There's another location that he's also been. But, usually he comes here. We have another team in the other location on the lookout for Arthur. If they pick up his scent they will notify us so that we can get you over there."

Well, that explained where Ethan, Daisy, Shane, and possibly Beto were. Gerald nodded his understanding.

Now that I knew I was looking for a nine year old male, I was able to search more efficiently. I flitted in and out of the heads around me, quickly moving on from those minds that clearly belonged to perverted adults. After meeting up at the ranch and being told who I would be working with tonight, we'd headed out and arrived at this location around nine. I'd ridden with Daisy and Ethan to the ranch at their insistence. I figured I'd better go along with it since I might have to fight with Logan about being there to find Arthur. However, Logan didn't even comment about me showing up after he'd told Ethan and Daisy to inform me that I wouldn't be needed for the takedown. He simply smirked as he greeted me.

It was about ten thirty as I was absentmindedly flipping through minds when I picked up on one that felt like that of a child. He was searching for someone. I honed in on the mind and realized he was frantically scenting the air in search of a specific scent. It was definitely a drainer, and it felt like a very despairing juvenile. Just like with Gerald, I could pick up his mind, but I couldn't tell where he was.

Sometimes I could tell where someone was because of the images I could see coming from their minds. Or, even if I wasn't familiar with a specific area but could see the mental images of another and compare them to what I saw in front of me, I could get some idea of their location. For example, if I knew someone was in a tall building and they showed images of looking out of a window, I could determine what floor they were likely to be on based on the view from the window. In the case of Arthur, I didn't see any of the images he was seeing, so I had no idea where he was.

"He's here, but I'm not sure where," I thought to Logan.

"Gerald, why don't you step out and see if you can scent your brother," Logan suggested, acting immediately on the information I provided. "Jordan, stay with him."

Jordan and I had not said a word to each other tonight other than to say a stiff hello. I sensed him wanting to say something, but I made sure he never had the opportunity. Thankfully he didn't try to press the issue by speaking out loud to me or in my head.

Gerald was out of the car in no time with Jordan right beside him. He immediately scented his brother and began thinking his name. Or, I thought he was simply thinking his name until I saw Logan and Grace's heads whip around at the same time in the direction Jordan and Gerald had gone. I couldn't hear a thing, but obviously they could.

"*Gerald?*" came the hopeful thoughts of the mind I'd been following. I guessed Arthur was speaking aloud also because the heads of Grace and Logan jerked around in another direction.

"*Yes, it's me, Arthur. Where are you?*" Gerald said excitedly. I decided to stay in Arthur's brain for a while since bouncing back and forth was making me dizzy.

"*Gerald! I thought you were dead!*" Arthur exclaimed feeling a deep relief and joy. He began to cry and his vision blurred.

"*Nope. I'm right here little brother,*" I heard Gerald's voice in Arthur's head. "*Just keep talking so we can find you.*"

193

I felt fear flicker in Arthur's mind and he stopped talking and walking.

"*He's afraid because you are there, Jordan,*" I warned. I wouldn't hesitate to speak to Jordan concerning the job. Any other conversation, however, was off limits.

"*Maybe you should explain to him who I am.*" I heard the words in Jordan's mind as he said them to Gerald. "*I'm sure he is scenting me too.*"

I felt a wave of dizziness again as I switched back to Arthur's mind to note his reaction. I wasn't sure that Jordan had spoken loud enough for Arthur to hear, but his reaction had not changed. He was warring between his feelings of wariness and his need to see his brother.

"*Arthur, do you remember the Alexander family that Mom and Dad used to talk to us about?*" came Gerald's words to me via Arthur's mind.

"*Yes,*" came Arthurs reply.

"*Well, they found me last night. I'm here with Jordan Alexander. They helped me find you. They are keeping me safe and helping me find you to keep you safe,*" Gerald explained.

"*I was so scared,*" Arthur said crying in relief and desperately seeking his brother.

"*I know. Just stay where you are and keep talking,*" Gerald said soothing his little brother.

Arthur wasn't saying much but his crying must have led them straight to him. In a few more moments they were together, and I was able to get out of everyone's heads. I let my head fall back against the headrest in the car and closed my eyes in an attempt to let my whole head rest. I heard Logan turn the car on and felt it begin to move. Moments later the doors were opening and Jordan, Gerald and another little boy, who looked the same as he had in Gerald's mind the night before, climbed in. Gerald was cradling the little boy as he cried.

Chapter 23

Once Arthur had been fed he was more composed. Logan had wanted to question him, but I cautioned him to not ask any leading questions. I suspected that he was as innocent as Gerald had insisted he was the night before. As Arthur began devouring his second helping of food, Logan eased into the questions.

"Arthur, it must have been very scary out there for you all by yourself. Gerald told us about your family. How did you escape those bad people?"

"I snuck out to the barn to wait for Gerald. When I saw some people had arrived, I started back to the house to see who they were. Only, I heard gunshots so I ran and hid down by the river," he explained as he shoveled food into his mouth.

"You weren't in the house?" Gerald asked looking up from his own plate.

"No. And then, when the bad men finally left, I went back to the house," he said putting his fork down and leaning back in his chair. His lip began to tremble and my heart broke for him. "Only, I couldn't go back in. I smelled blood. A lot of blood. So, I ran."

A look of pained relief flitted across Gerald's face before he looked down to hide his reaction from his brother. I knew he was thinking the same thing I was. Thank goodness Arthur hadn't gone back inside and seen his parents lying there in all of that carnage.

"So, how did you survive?" Daisy asked. "Where you out there by yourself all this time? Even at night?"

"No," he said, turning away with the beginnings of a shy smile after meeting Daisy's eyes. Cute. Daisy made him blush. "I found a few dogs to sleep with at night. I didn't have anything to eat so..."

He trailed off with a quick glance at me, and I caught the thought that flickered across his mind. He wasn't supposed to talk about being a drainer in front of me. I was a normal.

"So, what did you eat?" Gerald asked nervously, steeling himself for the answer. Arthur's eyes flicked to me again and then down uncomfortably.

"Nothing," he mumbled. "I said I didn't have anything to eat."

"It's ok, Arthur. I know about drainers and healers," I smiled at him. "But, you are right not to just talk freely in front of any of us normals. I think I am the only one who knows."

"Well," he said cautiously. "I don't kill animals or anything. I just figured if I stayed with the dogs at night they could help keep watch against danger. And, I drained some of their life force like I was taught to. But, I always left before the owners could wake up and catch me sleeping with the dogs."

I could feel the Alexander clan making it a point not to look at each other. And, from all I could tell, Arthur was telling the truth.

"So, all of the dogs were still alive when you left them?" I asked casually. I saw Gerald look at me sharply, but he remained quiet.

"Yes," he said with a frown. "But, one seemed a little too weak. I heard a boy calling him from the house right before I left, but the dog didn't move. I think I might have drained too much from him. I hope he was ok."

Arthur looked worried about the dog. As I monitored his mind, I saw the image of the last dog that had been brought in the clinic. The dog was definitely not alright, but I didn't think telling him that would be a good idea.

"So, what did you do after that?" I asked.

"I was walking and walking. Finally I was walking one night in this place where all these women seemed to be. It was pretty run down, but I figured it was because the women didn't have any men around to help them paint and stuff. And the men that where there always made big messes, and were drinking and leaving bottles and stuff everywhere. But, I felt safer there with the women. One of the women saw me and told me I could come and stay with her for the night. She fed me and even let me sleep right next to her. I was afraid to be outside at night, so I did. But, I made sure I left before the sun came up so that she wouldn't be able to call those child services people I heard her talking about. She had asked me if I was lost and I told her yes. She said these child service people could help me find my parents, but…well, I knew that they wouldn't find my parents."

"So each night you would stay with her?" Logan asked.

"No. I didn't think that would be a good idea. And, all I had to do was stand around for a while and one of the women would offer to take me home. I went home with someone different each time."

"Did you also take some of their life force?" Grace asked carefully.

"Yes!" he said sounding excited. "It was great. I'd never had anything like that before. But, I always made sure that I didn't take it all. I always left a little."

Grace nodded and plastered an unreadable expression on her face. One look at Gerald and I could see the horror on his face.

"Does he really think he left those women and dogs alive?" Came Logan's disturbed question in my head.

I nodded and sent my thoughts back to him. *"I don't think it's a good idea to tell him otherwise, either. He's been through enough, and he seems to be a sensitive kid. I don't know how well he could handle that."*

"Gerald can I talk with you for a minute?" Logan asked. "Come on down to my office with me for a moment. Lela, I think you should head on home and get some sleep. It's after midnight already."

I was more than happy to comply until Jordan insisted on taking me home. I didn't want to make a fuss in front of everyone, but I certainly didn't want to spend time with Jordan. Still, I said my goodbyes and headed out the door with Jordan. For a moment, I thought we were going to have another quiet ride home. But, then Jordan had to open his mouth and speak once we got a little distance away from the ranch.

"He wants you, Lela. It's obvious."

"I'm not talking to you about this, Jordan," I said evenly.

"Why? Because, you know it's the truth?" he countered.

"You mean to tell me if you had to do what he did last night, you wouldn't have had a physical reaction? I imagine actors get turned on during love scenes in a movie. It doesn't mean that they are going to do anything outside of the movie shoot. And, I'm sure their shoots aren't so violent, so they likely actually get turned on," I retorted.

"Do you know how bad of an analogy that is? Do you know how many of them probably do have affairs? Hollywood doesn't exactly have a good track record when it comes to relationships."

"I'm just saying he was just doing his job, and it wasn't easy for him or me. He didn't deserve to get punched by you," I said giving up trying to reason with him.

"Why are you trying to defend him? What the hell is really going on between the two of you?"

"Jordan, drop it. Ok?" I said firmly as he pulled into my driveway. "You can think whatever you want. I'm done. Clearly you don't believe there is nothing going on between Shane and me. So, if you really have that little trust in me and what's between us, then we clearly don't need to be together. I can't work like this."

I hopped out of the car and made my way to the door with Jordan on my heels. This time I didn't open the door. I turned to face him.

"What the hell are you saying, Lela?" he asked with a myriad of emotions flitting across his face.

"I'm saying I can't do this. I said I would give this a try. But, clearly I wasn't the only one with trust issues," I said looking him right in the eye. "I don't know what you want from me, but I'll be damned if I'm going to try and defend myself when I have done nothing wrong just because you have trust issues. And I sure as hell am not going to keep taking your innuendos and accusations. This is not working."

He stared at me with a stunned expression on his face. After a few moments, I realized he wasn't going to speak.

"Goodnight, Jordan," I said definitively and he took a couple of steps back as if I'd pushed him. I unlocked the door, stepped in and closed the door behind me with Jordan standing on the porch. Several minutes later, I heard the car engine start and the car pull slowly out of the driveway. That's when I slid down the door with my head in my hands. It hurt more than I was capable of describing that he would so accuse me of such a thing. Based on what? A violent acting performance? I didn't understand it at all, but it drudged up every self-protective instinct I had. This is why you didn't let people get close to you. Once you let them in, they could and would hurt you. They'd strike without thought or care and expect you to just accept the blows.

I wanted so badly to call Daisy. But, Daisy was Jordan's family. And this was why you didn't break the rule of dating the brothers or relatives of your friends. Only, I'd met Jordan first. Wasn't this a screwed up situation. I picked up my phone and dialed.

"Hey, Brat," came Blake's concerned voice.

"Hey," I said. I'd forgotten how late it was in my need to hear my brother's comforting voice.

"What's wrong?" he asked still sounding cautious.

"Nothing. I'm sorry. I just got in and didn't realize how late it was," I explained. "Did I wake you up?"

"No. I was up late working," he said. "Why are you getting in so late?"

"I was working on that other case with the Alexanders," I sighed.

"You sound…, different. Is everything alright?" Blake asked. He knew me too well for me to hide much from him.

"It's fine. It was just a really hard case," I hedged. "There were a few murders involved, and I found it all very disturbing."

"I can definitely see how murders could be disturbing," he agreed wryly. "Do you want to talk for a while? You know, to get your mind off of things?"

"I don't want to keep you up," I said trying to be considerate. I wanted nothing more than to talk to my brother. I wished he was here so I could sit on his lap like I did as a child and cry all over him.

"I'm not going to bed just yet. You've got half an hour. Start talking," he said with mock authority.

I talked to my brother for almost an hour. I didn't talk about Jordan or the case. I wanted to hear more about what he was doing at work and how his day had gone. He ended up telling me a few funny stories and some incredibly awful jokes that made me laugh. By the time I got off the phone with Blake I was at least settled enough to go to sleep.

Chapter 24

The next day was Saturday and Logan called to see if I could meet them all at the ranch at one in the afternoon.

"It seems we've solved one case only to open another," Logan was saying as we all sat around the conference room table. Jordan and I sat as far from each other as possible and avoided looking at each other. "Now that we know, and have put a stop to who was killing the men, women, and dogs, we have to find out who killed Gerald and Arthur's parents. So, I sent out a few feelers and we got a lead. Ricky, you want to explain?"

Ricky was another of the drainers I'd met on my first encounter with the Alexanders. I hadn't seen him lately though.

"Sure," Ricky said taking over. "Just on a hunch we went over to talk to our friend Kevin White to see if he could shed any light here. Fortunately, for us, he was able to shed a lot of light."

I shuddered at the name. Kevin White was the drainer who'd tried to kill me twice. He was the reason I'd come to know, and had fallen under the protection of, the Alexanders just a few short months back. The Alexanders had caught him when he'd kidnapped me and was trying to kill me. They'd arrived in the nick of time. I'd originally thought Kevin was dead. I'd somehow made the false assumption that Jordan, or one of the other Alexanders, had killed Kevin when they'd pulled him off of me. It wasn't until I was asked to assist on a kidnapping case with the Alexanders that I learned that Kevin was still very much alive.

Not only had I been asked to work with them on the case of a kidnapped banker who'd been abducted by Kevin's former organization, but my primary responsibility was to sit in on interrogations of Kevin to determine what he knew. I had sat less than fifteen feet away from him. It was a terrifying experience, yet I'd done it. And as a result we'd saved the banker.

"Turns out that Gerald and Arthur are Kevin's nephews," Ricky said bringing my thoughts back to the conference room.

"What?" Daisy cried.

"You've got to be joking," Ethan was saying.

"Yea. He and the father, Gerald Sr. were brothers," Ricky continued. "From all we can tell, Kevin's brother had no idea of what his big brother was up to. But, we already knew that Kevin also had a legitimate side to his life. Kevin was pretty devastated. He'd had no idea that his brother and sister-in-law were dead."

"Unbelievable," Ethan muttered.

"The only good news here is," Ricky went on, "remember Kevin's anonymous friend on the inside that was helping us locate properties before?"

"The one that led us to where Mr. Beck was being held hostage?" Beto asked.

"Yes. That's the one. He came through with some information for us. He released the information only after we promised to help him get out of the organization. After what's happened to Kevin, he wants out." Ricky explained. "He's given us the location where the leader who ordered the hit on Lela is supposed to be tonight. Apparently, this guy ordered Kevin's brother and family killed. He's got it in for Kevin since he figured out Kevin had to have helped us with the Beck case. Kevin's friend says he is supposed to meet with the boss tonight. We are setting it up to look like an ambush and he is supposed to get shot and taken by us."

"This is where you come in, Lela," Logan cut in turning to me. "We are supposed to meet with Kevin's man tonight. He's agreed to come to the holding facility where Kevin is being held. We want to go over the plan there, and we want you to be there to make sure they aren't leading *us* into an ambush."

"I can do that," I agreed quickly.

"After that, we want you on site," Logan continued. Out of the corner of my eye, I saw Jordan's jaw clench. "You won't be in any direct danger. As a matter of fact you will be well away from the fighting. We just need you there to assist us with what is going on once we storm the place. Any assistance you can provide will be helpful."

"Not a problem," I affirmed. "I can do that."

"Ok, you will be with Grace and Daisy. The rest of us will be going in," Logan announced. "Get some rest because there will probably be a lot of mind bouncing for the rest of the night once we meet with Kevin and his friend. We'll have Daisy and Grace pick you up at six."

Chapter 25

Once I arrived at the facility, I was quickly ushered into one of the interrogation observation rooms. I was hit with a case of déjà vu that made me shudder. The last time I was in this room, I listened to Kevin's interrogations in an effort to search his mind for information that would help us rescue a kidnap victim. This secret facility hiding in plain sight housed dangerous drainers and healers. No regular governmental law enforcement agency could possibly contain them. However, this was a governmental facility that had a special section for extremely dangerous criminals. The director of the facility was a healer and the staff was hand-picked. Anyone deemed too dangerous for the regular areas of the facility was placed in this top secret area. So, those high government officials that were that special brand of human like the Alexanders could house criminals here without the rest of the government, or world, finding out.

These interrogation rooms were sound proofed so that only those within the interrogation room and attached observation room could hear what was being said. Even other drainers or healers in the facility couldn't hear what went on in there.

Just like before, I was surrounded by several clothing articles to mask my scent. I was also wearing a combination of Grace and Daisy's clothes, just like before, to protect against Kevin and his friend picking up my scent as I was brought through the facility. Assuming they couldn't mask it all together, even if Kevin did pick up my scent, it would be mingled with the Alexanders. Since I had been under the protection of the Alexanders and mingled with them regularly the two times he'd tried to kill me, scenting me on them wouldn't raise any suspicions that I was actually there.

I took my place against the wall just beside the one way glass. I knew the minute that they walked in. This time, Kevin and his friend, Brent was the name I picked up in his mind, were escorted in by Ethan, Logan, Jordan, Beto and Ricky. I guess the guys weren't taking any chances with two of them.

"Do you have the layout?" Logan asked when everyone in the room was seated.

"Yes," Kevin said stiffly. Kevin was practically vibrating with unleased rage. He wanted nothing more than to kill everyone that had something to do with the deaths of his brother and his brother's family. Not being certain originally that Kevin hadn't had something to do with his brother's death, he hadn't been informed that his nephews were still alive. Not knowing who had killed the family, the Alexanders had thought it better that no one know that the boys were alive and being protected.

I switched to this Brent person's head just as he was laying out some sort of map.

"We are to meet here. Everyone will be in this room for dinner, except for the serving staff," Brent was saying. I had never seen this man before or heard his mind. I was curious to put a face to the mind but didn't dare step in view of the glass where Daisy and Grace were watching. Not that he would have necessarily been able to see me, but I wasn't taking any chances. He would definitely know that someone else was there.

His mind was surprisingly less disturbing than Kevin's. Actually Kevin seemed like a fairly rational individual the few times before that I'd been in his head. It was my previous experience of being on the receiving end of his homicidal tendencies that made it difficult for me to see him as anything but a monster. I had no idea what this Brent was like. Right now, he was disillusioned about this criminal organization he and Kevin were a part of. He was feeling that this leader that had killed Kevin's family had no loyalty to anyone. This Brent person was no longer willing to be part of an organization that saw him as expendable. Honor among thieves? Currently, all of his focus was on making sure this operation ran smoothly and he gained his freedom from this organization.

"The serving staff will be armed," Kevin was saying. "And, they will step in to protect Leonard."

"Yes, they will," Brent agreed. "I don't really know how many of them there will be. However, our best bet is if you guys come in when everyone is eating. Not expecting an attack, they will all likely be in the process of serving. That leaves only the outside guards that are really on alert. And they will be only on the lookout for someone approaching from the front. The back of the property is patrolled only by a passing guard. If you guys enter from here, it's a direct shot to the dining room where we will all be. The guards in the front will be coming in as soon as they are alerted to trouble. But, since it's not a big meeting, there shouldn't be more than about ten guards all together. They aren't expecting anything like this. They likely aren't expecting anything at all."

From what I could tell, both Brent and Kevin were just as eager for this mission to come off without a hitch. I continued to listen in on both of their minds throughout the planning session and only sensed grim determination.

"Leonard will likely sit here," Kevin was saying. "This is the most defensible position at the table. He never sits at the head of the table which has a clear shot from too many doors or windows."

"I've never been to one of these meetings actually. So I don't know where I'll be," Brent said.

"Which leads me to my next thought. There are only two reasons why Leonard would invite you to one of his dinner meetings," Kevin said in deep thought now. He was trying to weigh the possibilities of each of his theories. "Either they are on to you for some reason so they plan to take you out, or they want to promote you."

Kevin clearly had a twinge of unease about this. He was basically certain that Brent was on his side, but his suspicious nature had him questioning anyway. Popping over to Brent's head, it became very obvious that he was on Kevin's side. His mind was reeling at the idea that he might have actually been invited to the meeting to be killed. He knew it was an honor of sorts to be invited to the meeting. But, he'd never known that people were also killed at these meetings. No one ever knew about the meetings besides the invitees. And no one ever talked about the meetings besides the obvious survivors who were promoted. Part of being promoted would be knowing not to discuss any executions. And, since the members of the organization worked in anonymous cells, no one would know that anyone was taken out from another cell of the organization.

We learned during the kidnapping investigation that the only reason why Kevin and Brent knew each other was because they were leaders of their own cells. Sometimes the leaders were brought together but never encouraged to intermingle much. They were given their orders and they were not allowed to tell anyone else what those orders were, not even the other cell leaders in attendance. Secrecy was very strict. So, even when members of another cell were taken out and executed, the leaders of other cells often had no idea what had actually happened to them. They were just the secret target of another cell. Brent and Kevin had formed a sort of friendship however. So, when Brent noticed suspicious activity surrounding Kevin's cell and Kevin went missing, he got suspicious. Kevin had also covertly reached out to Brent for help and the two had ended up working with the Alexanders to not only help save Kevin, but rescue a kidnap victim.

"Well, how would I know what they plan to do?" Brent said sounding a bit uneasy. His mind had gone into a small panic before he began to force himself to stay calm so he could think. He had all intentions of making it out alive.

"You won't until you sit down to eat," Kevin said cautiously. "If you are there for a promotion you will be in a defensible position. If not, you will be in the easiest location for someone to take you out."

I noticed Kevin did not point these positions out. However, I was fairly certain that Brent was on the up and up here. There wasn't a hint in his mind about an ulterior motive. I sent my concluding thoughts on Brent to the minds of the Alexander team in the room.

"Ok. I think we have everything. I need to confer with my men. Brent, when the fighting starts, you will be one of the first ones hit. You will be tranqued however. That will take you out of harm's way as much as possible until we have things under control and can extract you."

"You are going to drug me?" He asked indignantly.

"Yes. If we left you coherent they would expect you to fight. We just need to make sure you look like you've been shot with a regular bullet. So expect to be hit."

He didn't like it, but he agreed. Once Kevin was taken away and Brent left to prepare for his meeting, the Alexanders gathered in the little observation room with Grace, Daisy, and me.

"I didn't detect anything amiss," I explained. "Kevin is seething with rage over his brother's death. He really wants to be there to kill Leonard himself. And, Brent just wants out. That's all I picked up."

"That's good. I got the impression though, that Kevin was a little unsure about Brent," Jordan said looking at me with his professional face. This face I could handle.

"He is. Only, he doesn't have any reason or gut instinct telling him to be unsure about Brent. It's just appears to be his cautious nature to question if he should be trusting him. He was more eager to trust him but cautioning himself to never trust anyone entirely."

"Ok, I'm going to give some last minute instructions to our outside tactical team. We can't take the outside guards out without the people inside knowing what's going on at the same time. So, what I'll be looking for from you, Lela, is knowing where everyone is before we go in. That way, team two can take out the outside guards while we secure the inside."

"I'll do my best," I said feeling the weight of the responsibility of my task. If I didn't get it right, someone could get hurt.

"Ethan will be leading team two and the rest of us here will be going inside with me. So, to make it easier on you, Ethan and I will be wearing these trusty little goggles," Logan grinned holding up a pair of tactical goggles. "You'll only need to send a text with the word 'go'. That way it will flash across our vision at the same time so that we can give our teams the signal at the same time. We need this to be precise and don't want any delay from you having to bounce from one mind to another. In the meantime, any other communication you need to give us, you can direct to me or Ethan."

"Got it," I said feeling my stress levels rise. Oh, boy. I was having performance anxiety or something.

Chapter 26

Once we were all in position, I visually scanned the house at the end of the street. I had to use night vision goggles to get a good feel for the place while everyone else could use their regular eyes. Once I had the lay of the land, I probed around the back of the house where I couldn't see. There was one lowly guard out there. Flitting through the minds of the guards, none of them where really on any type of alert. They weren't expecting anything to happen tonight. This was just routine. I didn't give these impressions to Ethan and Logan, however. I figured the more on alert they were the better.

I tried very hard not to think about Logan, Jordan, Beto, and Ricky going inside. They would be in the most danger. If anything happened to any of them, I don't know how I would handle that. They'd all come to mean so much to me. And, I refused to let myself even think about losing Jordan. Even though his current caveman, dictatorial behavior had me backing out of our relationship, it didn't mean that I didn't still care for him deeply. I just refused to allow him to start treating me like his possession. I'd been making decisions for myself for quite some time now. The very idea that he thought he could tell me what I could and could not do, and act like he owned me or something in front of his family, had every fiber of my being rebelling. Then his jealousy and accusations. I hadn't seen any of this coming. I could never survive or function in this type of relationship. Compromise, disagreement, and discussion were one thing. Dictating, ordering, accusations, and possession of me were something completely different.

The guard at the back began to make his way back to the front of the house leaving the back completely unguarded. I refocused my attention. Apparently, they were taking turns making their rounds to the back every few minutes and this was the time to act. Daisy and Grace were sitting quietly in the front of the SUV watching. We were roughly a mile away and they were sitting as still as stones. We'd arrived long before the guards showed up so they wouldn't see a car drive up and no one get out further up the street. Once the guard made his way to the side of the house I pressed the send button, sending the text that would move both teams into action.

"Guard headed your way from the back of the house on your right," I thought to Ethan. I knew Logan's team would have a visual of the guard leaving, and knew the guard could turn back if he chose to once the commotion started. We'd already confirmed that there were nine guards. Thankfully, the house was not very large. So, while there were a few guards right in front, the others were posted to the front but on either side where the neighboring houses were joined.

Suddenly there was a flurry of movement that I couldn't understand. I knew that both teams had moved in. I tried to stay in Logan's head to keep up with what was going on. They stormed the room, crashing through the glass doors, but everyone was moving so fast I couldn't tell what was going on even from Logan's mind. He glanced at something and then noted that Brent was down. In a matter of seconds it all seemed to be over.

"Ethan's hit," Daisy said out loud just as Logan jerked his head around.

"Oh, God," I said just as Logan opened fire in a flash of movement I couldn't follow.

"What happened?" Grace asked. Both she and Daisy turned towards me. "What's happening inside?"

"There are more in the hall and the kitchen!" I shouted to Logan and Ethan in their minds. They immediately moved. I winced from the pain of jumping from mind to mind so quickly, but I didn't dare lose contact. When the smoke cleared, Ethan and Logan were still standing, though seeing Ethan through Logan's eyes, I could see Ethan was bleeding.

"What the hell happened," Grace gritted out pulling me from Logan's head.

"Ricky was hit. He needs help," I said quickly just as Grace's phone rang. Grace hit the speaker button.

"Grace, we need you here now," came Jordan's voice. "Ricky was hit and he's bleeding out. Ethan's hit and can't help much when he's injured."

"I'm on my way," Grace said turning the engine on and barreling down the street. The car had barely come to a stop before she and Daisy were out of the car.

They were back in a flash, but this time with Ethan and Jordan carrying Ricky to the car.

"We don't have time to wait for a proper transport. Jordan you have to drive. Ethan needs to heal himself, I can't help him right now," Grace was saying as they were loading Ricky in the car. I scrambled into the front seat to get out of the way and ended up between Ethan and Jordan. "Daisy try to stop the bleeding while I try to repair some of the damage. I can't heal him fast enough on my own, hand me my medical bag."

"He's lost a lot of blood," Ethan was saying from the front seat as Jordan threw the car into gear and peeled out onto the street. I was thrown against Ethan's injury and he and Ricky groaned at the same time. That was when I realized Ricky was still conscious. He had a painful grimace on his face and his eyes where squeezed tightly shut.

"Jordan, try not to jostle us too much," Grace ordered from the backseat.

"Sorry," Jordan apologized grimly.

Once we made it to the ranch, Ricky was swiftly moved to Grace's surgery. There was nothing for me to do but wait. Ethan, Daisy, and Jordan had followed Ricky and Grace into the surgery. I found my way to the dining hall and wasn't surprised to find food being set out by the kitchen staff. After what seemed like forever, Ethan came out and found me picking over some pasta salad.

"Logan and the rest of them are here," he said sitting down beside me. "Ricky is going to be fine. Grace says that she stopped the bleeding and had to do some immediate surgery. She made me help."

I sighed with relief.

"I didn't know you had some nursing skills," I said absently.

"I don't. But the little bit of healing ability I have was needed," he said looking haggard. Still, I could tell his wound looked better.

"I guess there was a lot of mess to clean up at the house. I'd hate to have that job," I said still feeling shell shocked at all the carnage of the evening.

"Not too much of a mess," Ethan said quizzically.

"What about all of those bodies?" I asked with a shudder. I had clearly stepped out of my perfectly normal life into a spy movie after meeting the Alexanders.

"Lela, we were shooting tranquilizers. Didn't we tell you before that we don't kill suspects unless we have to?" Ethan asked looking amused.

"Tranquilizers?" I asked confused.

"Logan and I were the only ones with live ammo. And, Leonard was the only one we actually killed when he shot Ricky. The two other people we actually shot, we didn't kill."

"Oh," I said before thinking of another question. "So what's going to happen to Gerald and Arthur?"

"Well, from what I understand they do have some cousins they can live with out of state. But, right now, they are still being kept under wraps until we can be positive that they aren't in any danger from anyone else in Kevin's organization," Ethan explained.

"Those poor kids," I said trying not to remember all of their pain I'd felt.

"Yea. Grace is making sure they are getting some psychiatric counselling and being taken care of until we can get them back with family," Ethan agreed. "They've been through a lot. But, Logan is fairly sure that they won't be prosecuted for murder. They would just be more victims in the system."

Logan came in then to talk to me. Even he looked more haggard then I'd ever seen him look.

"I know you need to get home and get some rest, but I wanted to talk to you about your work situation," he began as he lowered himself into the chair next to me. "I'll be brief and you can go home and think on it. I know I can't ask you to leave Hanley's and come and work for us full time. But, I'm hoping there will be a way that we can have you on a more part-time basis. Do you think he will go for you splitting your position with someone else? I know it's a lot to ask. And of course we will take you however we can get you. You are a valuable asset to us. Go home and think about it. You don't have to give me any decision now. Just tell me you'll think about it."

"What exactly are you asking me, Logan?" I asked. He had thrown everything out so fast, I wasn't clear on just what he was trying to say.

"Working these double shifts with two jobs is taking its toll on you," Logan said on a tired smile. "I'd love to have you full-time, but I'm hoping to at least get you to maybe go part-time at Hanley's. You are a part of our team here. Of course, we will honor whatever you decide to do. But, I want you to at least think about it. We'll pay you enough to make it worth your while. For now, just say you'll think about it."

"I'll think about it," I said with a tired smile of my own as Logan stood. I stood as well.

"Good," Logan nodded and then gave me a quick hug. "Great work, Lela. I'll have Daisy drive you home."

"Daisy is still in with Grace," came Jordan's voice from the open doorway. "I'll drive you home."

"That's ok," I said as Jordan came into view. "I can wait on Daisy."

"I really need to talk to you," Jordan said quietly. He didn't take his eyes off of me as Logan and I headed towards the door and him.

"I'll just go check on Ricky," Logan said hastily excusing himself. He disappeared down the hall leaving me alone with Jordan.

"Grace said he'll be fine in a few days," Jordan called to his brother as Logan made his way rapidly away from us.

"Jordan, I don't want to fight with you," I said with a frown and walked past him to follow Logan.

"I just want to talk," Jordan said falling into step beside me.

"I don't want to talk either," I said trying to control my frustration. "I'm tired. I'm physically and mentally overwhelmed. I just can't do this-"

"I'm sorry," Jordan stated cutting me off. Taking advantage of my momentary speechlessness, he grabbed my elbow and escorted me out of the house and down to his waiting SUV. Fine. I would just listen. I didn't have to engage. I could let Jordan say what he had to say and be home in about twenty minutes. It was a fair trade. He opened my door for me and I slid inside. Once we were a few minutes away from the ranch, he broke the tense silence between us.

"I'm sorry, Lela," Jordan said again. He paused for a moment but continued when I said nothing. "I know you are really angry with me. And, I know I got a little unreasonable."

"What do you want me to say?" I asked uncomfortably.

"I want to know that you accept my apology for starters." He glanced at me and then shifted his gaze back to the dark road.

"I do, Jordan," I said sincerely. "I accept your apology."

"But, you're still angry with me." It was said as a statement.

"No. I'm actually not angry," I admitted. "I was before. But, I'm not anymore."

"Why do I still feel like you are putting up walls between us," Jordan asked gingerly.

"I'm not putting up walls. I'm just understanding why this is not a good idea."

"You mean us, right? You're trying to say you and I being together isn't a good idea?"

"Yes, Jordan. That's what I'm saying," I said after a long exhale.

"It was just a disagreement, Lela."

"No, Jordan it wasn't. Being told you disagree is a disagreement," I began coolly. "Being told you'd rather I didn't do something, or asking to discuss something would constitute a disagreement. Being told what I can and cannot do is not a disagreement. Being accused of basically cheating on you is not a disagreement. Being talked to like a child in front of your family and colleagues is not a disagreement."

Jordan was quiet for a moment as we pulled onto my street and into the driveway. He turned the engine off and turned towards me.

"I was wrong. I should never have accused you. I honestly don't believe you would do that to me," he said stoically. "I was reacting to the fact that I know Shane is very attracted to you. I also know that you are attracted to him. Seeing him all over you like that, touching you, it sent me over the edge. I let my own jealousy take over and…"

He trailed off.

"Jordan, it's late. I need to sleep," I said pulling my car door open. He made to get out but I stopped him. "No. Don't walk me to my door. I'm going to go inside now and get ready for bed. We can talk another day. I just can't do this right now."

"Promise me we'll talk tomorrow," Jordan commanded. Then he took in my sardonic face and added, "Please."

"We will talk. I can't guarantee it will be tomorrow," I said stubbornly. He nodded.

"One last question. Can we agree to work together without it being weird or difficult?" he asked.

"Yes. I can agree to that," I said. Something in the back of my mind told me that this was crucial for Jordan, and I didn't think it had anything to do with work. In fact, I thought it was something calculated to thwart my attempts at putting distance between us that had him asking the question.

"Goodnight, Lela."

"Goodnight, Jordan."

I wasn't sure what else to say. I felt there had been a question in his comment about Shane, but I wouldn't lie and say that I didn't find Shane attractive, because I did. I wouldn't have kissed him those few weeks ago if I didn't. But, I found a lot of men attractive. There's a huge difference in finding someone attractive and actually wanting them. I didn't want Shane. But, I couldn't change the past, nor did I regret it. When I'd kissed

Shane, I was not in any type of relationship with Jordan. I hadn't even seen him in six weeks. But, Jordan was, and had been, the one that I wanted. However, I couldn't fight his personal demons for him. I'd told him time and time again that nothing besides that kiss had ever went on between Shane and me. I wouldn't go any further into a relationship with someone who didn't trust me. Especially considering that if I continued to work with the Alexanders, then I would have to work with both Jordan and Shane to some capacity.

I wasn't sure what portion of Logan's offer I was going to choose. The only thing that I was certain about was that I would continue to work with the Alexanders. So, maybe breaking off this relationship with Jordan now was the best thing. Mixing business and pleasure was never a good idea. Although, even as I thought about breaking things off completely, there was a voice in the back of my mind telling me that it would never work. If I wasn't able to resist Jordan before, then I certainly wouldn't be able to resist him now. But, if I broke things off now and he didn't pursue it, then perhaps things would go smoothly.

For now, I wasn't ready to give in. I needed time and space. I needed to think and regroup. So now, I was going to go inside, sleep alone in my bed and let tomorrow take care of itself.

Made in the USA
San Bernardino, CA
18 July 2014